Thief of the Sunshine Yellow

ANNA LAWRIE

Copyright © 2016 Anna Lawrie

All rights reserved.

ISBN:153919616X
ISBN-13:9781539196167

DEDICATION

This book is dedicated to my husband Graeme Lawrie who keeps me sane (while trying not to look too worried that I may have written any part of his personality into one of my characters).

My aim was to weave a true love story: splendorous yet very tangible. I feel very lucky that in research terms I started from a position of great advantage.

I would also like to mention my children Joe and Finn: Dr Seuss really did know what he was talking about when he conceived a Grinch with a heart that grew three sizes. I love you all.

I am extremely fortunate to be supported by an incredibly kind family and loyal friends: my Welsh, French, English, Zimbabwean and Manx contingents, you know who you are.

CONTENTS

	Acknowledgements	i
1	Fate	Pg 3
2	Insincerity	Pg 15
3	Severance	Pg 41
4	Inadequacy	Pg 55
5	Bliss	Pg 74
6	Disappointment	Pg 86
7	Pretence	Pg 116
8	Triumph & Hopelessness	Pg 140
9	Wisdom	Pg 165
10	Misinterpretation	Pg 193
11	Anger	Pg 214
12	Love	Pg 224
13	Fulfilment	Pg 237

ACKNOWLEDGEMENTS

My sole acknowledgement is to my editor and super-mum Sue Heppenstall, without whom I would certainly still be fixing syntax, agonizing over plot points and searching for interesting character names.

She may feel compelled to give her own sub-acknowledgement to my Dad, who occasionally supplied the odd word I was searching for, with lazy but exact insightfulness. And maybe another little one to her sister, my Auntie Barb, who badgered me to write the ending after she had read the start.

1 FATE

A miniature yet realistic imitation of the *Spreuerbrücke* wooden bridge originally built on Earth in 1408, complete with ornate tile roof, currently zig-zags its way across a stagnant body of water in the conservation park at one end of the seventeenth Lunar Protectorate Dome. It is exactly to scale with its European original in all but one insignificant detail. One plank of wood which makes up the walkway is seven millimetres too short, and had to be screwed at a different angle, a decision made by the harassed foreman eleven years previously in order to make a deadline due in four days. The walkway is suspended just above the water level, and has withstood over 100, 000 pairs of feet trudging its boards, mostly school trips and tourists, coming to admire the wildlife in the park.

The Conservation Park makes impressive use of artificial lighting to cope with the 178 days of the year that fall during lunar nights, each one of which spans a depressing fifteen earth days. The first day of April in the year 2437 however, was the start of a lunar day and was therefore most welcomingly lit by natural rays of light. At midday, one small screw at the end of the shortest of the planks of wood making up the miniature *Spreuerbrücke*, worked itself loose, and plopped, unobserved, into the murky pond below, allowing a microscopic amount of lateral translation in the plank. The sideways movement of this one segment was just enough to slowly loosen the two remaining screws, a process taking exactly thirty one days and four minutes.

* * *

Edytha turned her face away from the glare of the orange tinted synth-sunlight, reminiscing of the days when she didn't have to worry about adding to the wrinkles around her eyes. 'Don't know why I bother,' she grumbled, barely looking up at the man to whom this comment was aimed.

'If you are talking to me, let's hope you're not expecting reply.' Oszkár didn't attempt to disguise his Russian accent to his wife of nearly seventy years.

'When do I ever expect reply from you – *Padlo*!' She cursed him under her breath as she walked alongside the waterway known as W1346. Oszkár would never willingly use public transport: a cynic at heart, he had a lifetime's mistrust of public transport and governmental population mapping, which, he claimed to anyone who was willing to listen, were inextricably linked.

'Padlo am I? Ho! We shall see.' Oszkár stopped to rub his knee, and his wife overtook him on the narrow path with barely concealed tutting.

'If you let them take a look at you in hospital you would have new knee! Superstitious old goat!' A line of sleek black hydropods swept past them with a soft whirring, the slapping of the water hitting the embankment making more noise than the engines themselves.

'Hunngh! The rich, and their obsession with black pods. Looks more like a funeral procession if you ask me.'

'No-one ask you Oszkár, no-one ever ask you, but still you talk.'

Oszkár continued undeterred. 'If you knew what micro trackers they can install in new knees, you wouldn't be so eager for me to have one. Hah! If Titan dome government knew that you had helped destroy their offices in 2396, you would not be so welcome.'

'It was 2397, and was done under old identity, as well you know. You should trust the system, Oszkár…trust system and get new knee.'

'I'm far too old for robotic nonsense. I could be dead in a week, and would waste it, trying to figure out new neural connections. No, I will walk in the joints God gave me.'

'Well, walk then, and stop grumbling about your God-given joints.' Edytha raised her eyes to heaven, muttering about maggoty old men, outstripping her husband by so much, that when she turned the corner into her chalk gravel front yard, he could no longer be seen.

Their house was situated in Diakon ST25G8, a settlement within the Titan dome, orbiting at just over one million kilometres above Saturn. The orange clouds gave everything a slight glow, which sometimes tricked vacationers into thinking it was warmer than it was. Not that Diakon got many tourists. Titan Dome was a little too isolated and rural for tourists in general, and Diakon was a particularly boring community within it, boasting of little more than its white wooden houses and dusty roads. This was why they had chosen it of course. 'The system' as they tended to call anything to do with their old jobs and way of life, had chosen their house, issued their new passes, and re-written their history, so that they could enjoy an uncomplicated retirement. Edytha often wondered if Oszkár would have preferred their life to have remained complicated, and died doing what he loved, like so many others, rather than grumbling away the rest of his existence in a nowhere settlement.

Edytha turned the dial on the window frame two notches to darken the glass, ensured the seal around the house was unbroken and tapped the point on her skull where the optic nerve implant resided. The 'plant connected wirelessly with the small hub hidden beneath the kitchen surface and the semi-translucent screen image blinked into life, partly obscuring her view of the kitchen. She willed the cursor across the screen and activated their link to the government grid. It was a highly secure system, and they only used it to keep abreast of the latest political developments and to check every day that their identities remained protected.

'What in hell's name are you doing in broad light of day?' Oszkár snapped as he walked in to the kitchen.

'Checking FTTs. Quiet Oszkár I have just seen something.'

'Opening computer with door unlocked is nonsensical, as well you know, and never cease to shout at me for, when I do it!' Oszkár insisted.

'Door would not have opened without your fingerprints, so stop your worrying. Anyway – look at this!'

'That print-lock mechanism is usually my argument, Edytha. Now you have no come-back when I next use it! Hah!'

'Oszkár will you shut up and look at this! You told me I imagined the last one, but look – there is definitely FTT waiting to be opened from a stranger here. How would they know this address?' Edytha demanded, a frown hovering on her face, wondering if it would be needed or not.

'It will be a glitch Edytha, it won't be for me. Out of my way now, I will see to it…and make me drink will you? My knee is abysmal.'

'As if drink will help your knee – make it yourself. When you learn to ask nicely I might consider it. I have work to do Oszkár, I don't have time to be your maid!' Edytha whisked herself out of the room, not certain if her outrage was real or mock. Either way, being left on his own to think about it was no bad thing.

'Work! Hah! Did nobody tell you we retired?' Oszkár shouted to her, not caring whether she heard or not. She knew he was joking, so why did she have to turn it into yet another melodrama?

Edytha took one deep steadying breath. What did that foul-mouthed excuse for a husband know about running a household? When was the last time he weeded the vegetable run, or washed his own clothes, or arranged for the tank to be voided? He had no idea. He stared at his computer screen most days, God knows why, probably wishing for a life he no longer had, probably wishing he wasn't stuck in some God-forsaken town with only his wife for company.

Oszkár whistled through his teeth until the stomping feet disappeared from ear-shot then opened his latest FTT. Retirement came more easily for some than others... He scanned it quickly, one ear to the garden at all times. 'No, no, no.' He grumbled. And then a little further on: 'Useless!' He sighed the air out past his teeth with audible dissatisfaction. 'So much promise...and yet...such little common sense.'

He wrote a terse reply: 'Negative. Leave all exit strategies to me. As discussed leave object in parcel at scene. This is a necessary...' Oszkár paused, searching for the correct term in English...something to do with running goats or maybe red fish? No matter. 'This is necessary to repair the damage you did to our plan when you chose a location involving people you know. When you have the item, send to me immediately as per previous communication.'

He chuckled a little as he set up a devilish encryption, and shut down the screen before rubbing his hands together in glee.

*   *   *

April 31st was a day much anticipated by Miss Robertot's Class as they were going on a field trip. Tad knew, by quiet observation, that classes in St Catherine's Intermediate School only went on one trip each term. He knew lots of things like that. He knew that there was blue sticker spray holding the caterpillar collage to the wall to his left, but red sticker spray held the planet paintings to the wall on his right. He knew that his Dad's shoe had a glittery purple blob of paint on the sole from when they had decorated his room at the end of the school holidays. He knew that his Dad took the 6R pod to work and his mum took the 6R and then the 8A circular. Today, he sat on one of the yellow and green school pods, listening to the sound of Miss Robertot's voice transmitting from the front-most pod.

'When we get to the park, you will line up in your pairs and follow me down to the meadow. Each pair should already be carrying their square metre.'

Tad looked down to his blue polycarbonate square, the furthest corner currently being tapped repeatedly by the swinging foot of his partner, Frel. Frel was in fact named Jack Frellish, but within a week of starting school his surname was set, in true schoolboy fashion, as his nickname.

Tad opened his bag and inspected his packed lunch warily. 'What is it this time?' Frel enquired, grinning.

'I think it's buckwheat bread today,' Tad paused to prise apart the two slices, 'and French beans inside.

'Beans! Is that all you've got? She's losing her touch: that's almost normal!' Frel screwed his face up into a disappointed scowl, his top lip curling up.
'Hang on,' Tad lifted the sandwich up to his nose and sniffed in a full lung of air, 'I knew it! I have French beans with sweet chestnut spread today.'

'Cool! Let me taste – I wanna see how nasty it is!' Frel made a grab for the sandwich, sending the square metre flying, where it narrowly avoided a pair of girls' shins. They turned to glare, one of the girls craning her neck to get in her fair share of the indignation.

The two boys looked at each other with eyes wide and half a scared smile each, then collapsed into a fit of giggles. They felt the pods slosh to a stop, and pushed past the girls to get out onto the sunny wharf first.

Tad smiled to see a small puddle glinting in the sunshine and wondered if he had time to execute his plan before the teacher moved towards the back of the line. Yes. He planted his foot into the centre of the pool, at an angle. The small shower of water landed discreetly on the bare calves of his friend, but not willing to be outdone, Frel wiped the water off his legs with both hands and made a lunge to smear it on Tad's face.

'Jack Frellish?' Miss Robertot asked for the second time, looking up from her register.

'Yes, miss.' Frel schooled his face into an unreadable mask, but a little of the smile crept through, and a shadow of mischievousness still lurked about his eyes.

No intermediate school teacher of six years' experience, especially one of Miss Robertot's calibre, would fail to see past the angelic face to the naughty glee behind it, but today was their day out, so she let it slide. 'Pay attention boys, or we will be standing by the pod stop all day!'

'Yes, miss.' Frel bent his head as if in submission but instead sneaked a sideways look at Tad to share a grin with him, before looking back to the floor with lips pressed tightly together, suppressing the need to smile.

Tad waited for his name, staring at the skyline in a dome-centre direction. He could just make out the three white peaks of the Interstellar Parc where his Dad worked, and that made him smile; he would tell him tonight how close he had been.

Bracq Launay was employed as second engineer for the massive conglomerate that was 'Interstellar Parcs', in the New Elveden Forest Hotel. The forest in question was barely a grove, but Interstellar Parcs liked all their hotels to preserve the links to humanity's rich natural past: it was part of the original marketing apparently.

Bracq was at that precise moment tending to the bio-swim-pool, raking the grass covering to ensure maximum softness for their valued customers. He was always careful to put any stray Therran seeds or water hyacinth strands back into the end section of the pool, which the water flowed through for purification, and any toads or bogbean flowers were placed back in to the marsh section to the left. It was hard labour most of the day, but his jobs were varied, and he enjoyed the work.

He had to remind himself sometimes how much he enjoyed coming to work, when the automatic bank updates revealed how much their outgoings threatened to overtake their earnings. His male pride told him he should be earning more than, or at the very least equal to his wife, not less. He didn't want to hear how women had, on average 5% higher earnings than men, it didn't make him feel any better. What he wanted was to step back in time twenty odd years and shake himself by the shoulders when he made the decision to leave school at fifteen. At the time vocation training seemed the intelligent way forward; you 'earned as you learned', as they said in the slogans. Now, his life seemed distinctly lacking in possibilities. He didn't regret it...how could you regret having a beautiful wife and a boy like Tad? But it was true what people said, the boy wasn't well timed. He had arrived at about the same time as Bracq's one big break. Or rather, the one big break that got away. Ymarise had told him to go for it. 'How many times does something like this come along?' she had said. And, as it turned out, 'not very often' was the answer. His wife had argued that if he pulled it off, they could afford to have another child, to give Tadelesh a sister, maybe. But the opposite was unthinkable…losing their house in the dome that they had worked so hard for, having to go back to Earth: underprivileged, violent, overpopulated planet that it was. Bracq knew they needed a stable income, when a child was involved. He just couldn't live with the idea of risking his only son's way of life, future health even, by taking a chance on that job. So he had stayed with Interstellar Parcs.

And they had never done badly by him, his wage was increased every year, and most years the increases beat the inflation rate. He had got a promotion from third to second engineer six years ago, and it was just unlucky that the first engineer was happy in his job, and didn't want to leave it anytime soon. So life wasn't really that bad…and he really did enjoy his job: raking the grass under the surface of the water, with the sun warming your back – who could ask for more?

His son also liked to work most of the time, despite getting into some kind of trouble most days. He and Frel were sitting cross legged in a meadow, with the sun on their backs (and their teacher out of ear shot) enjoying the freedom of choosing to work rather than being made to. Their two faces were supported three inches off the floor, chins resting on hands, with bony elbows positioned on dry mud: a position which amuses most adults in its flexible impossibility. A notepad lay between them with three columns entitled 'original earth animals', 'genetically engineered moon animals' and 'mutant animals'.

'I can't see any animals apart from that bug that just flew away,' Tad complained. 'Does that count?'

'Maybe we were supposed to be counting plants?' Frel looked uncertainly at Tad, sitting up to locate their teacher. 'Miiiiiiss?' He asked in the age-old three syllable version of the word.

'Yes Jack?' Miss Robertot shielded her eyes from the sun and projected her voice.

Both boys rolled their eyes at the formal form of his name. 'We can't do it miss,' Tad shouted back. He bit his lip as he saw their teacher pick up her clipboard and stride out towards them.

'Let's see what you've found so far boys.' She urged gently, crouching between them.

Tad held up their paper and watched as the teacher's green pen scratched a few times, replacing the word 'animals' wherever it appeared with 'plants'. Tad looked at the pen, remembering where he had last seen it poking out from behind the busy-lizzy in their classroom. He wondered whether it was the same pen, or a replacement for the lost one next to the busy-lizzy.

Miss Robertot smiled and handed the black plastic pad back, 'That might make things a little easier for you. Remember, I need you to hand these in by the end of today, so I can upload them to the school.'

''S'miss' two voices chorused, heads once again bent to the

floor, immersed in their square metre of wildlife.

The rest of the day went by for Tad in a happy blur. As always, when he was enjoying himself, the time flew by twice as quickly. Tad had enjoyed working out of doors, and he thought his father would be happy with his end of term report as he and Frel had both been praised today for their effort. They trailed at the back as the group made their way back to the pods, to make up for being so good with their work, and thus earning each other's respect once again. Frel jumped with two feet on each plank as they crossed the bridge over the boggy patch of water, making a game out of it.

'I bet you can't do it backwards!' Frel taunted.

'I bet *you* can't!' Tad grinned until he felt the sickening feeling in his stomach of sudden movement downwards, his right foot falling through a plank that had slipped sideways, and then felt his blood drain rapidly out of his face and lips as he heard the sickening crunch of the bones in his left ankle being unable to resist the torsion of the position he was in.

It happened in a second, but time seemed to spin itself out to allow Tad to hear Frel screaming for their teacher, to give him time enough to see the exact way that his friend's ankle sock had bunched up into sort of the shape of a bird's foot, and time to feel scared of the amount of pain he was in, before fainting away with one leg dangling beneath the bridge, his shoe grazing the water surface.

2 INSINCERITY

A sleek line of black pods brought Tuula, her mother, her father, their PAs and various attendants to a polished marble building in New Manhattan, Europa's only limited access party town for society's elite. Tuula knew everyone that would be at tonight's charity ball. She had grown up knowing the mayor as Uncle El, his wife as Auntie Dune, and she had played bat-and-ball in the garden with his second wife Cailly, wearing her new orange wetsuit so she could run and dive into the artificial waterfall pool straight afterwards. Artur Litton-Strackey and Giles Brandforth she had seen naked in her paddling pool, and yet they still treated her as a slightly inferior breed, being two years her senior. One of these days she would remind them of her finals scores and watch their sneers disappear.

'Saphia! Whoohoo!' Dune called to Tuula's mother from across the room, and Tuula watched as Saphia craned her neck this way and that without seeing the owner of the voice even though she was standing in irritating full view.

'Saphie! Over here darling!' The woman continued in the same loud tones, refusing to walk the small distance across the floor to diminish the attention they were receiving.

'Oh Dune! How wonderful!' Her mother finally caught on to the situation, 'Look Tuula, Auntie Dune is here! Doesn't she just look out of this world?'

'Preposterous, more like.' Tuula muttered under her breath, knowing her mother would be too caught up in her social duties to expect an answer to her loudly spoken rhetoric. Sure enough, Saphia continued in the same vein, finally making it to Dune's side and consequently eliminating the necessity to share her obsequiousness with the entire room.

Her father had made a bee line for the drinks stand where a number of men were clustered, feet wide apart and hands thrust in pockets or behind backs, asserting their wealth and importance to the room as surely as the women did. Tuula followed him and reached past Ziedrich, Kerq and Yer to get a drink. She picked a frosted glass with a deep purple liquor settling heavily at the bottom, boasting its potency in smell and viscosity. She sipped at it warily and was surprised by the delicacy of taste. Mariposa Eastman obviously knew how to organise a good bash...or her party planner did, Tuula thought cynically. Talking of Mariposa, she was making her entrance, her fingers delicately resting on Uncle El's arm like a leech. Tuula scanned the room for Cailly but to no avail. The mayor caught her looking and shrugged his shoulders. Tuula made a 'never mind' expression back; the party had just gone down another notch in her estimation...not that she would be staying that long anyway.

She saw Bizelle leaning backwards ungracefully against a wall with a drink in each hand and an empty one on the sill behind her. Normally she would avoid all the Eastman's like the plague, but just this once, she could see a use to talking with this emaciated, under-confident addict. Tuula lifted an eyebrow, smiled slightly in her direction, but still getting no response, decided to take the plunge and head over there.

'Bizelle!' Tuula greeted, wondering how best to pierce the shroud of self-pity surrounding the girl, 'I wasn't sure you'd be here tonight!'

'My mother is organising this party. It doesn't take a genius to work out I might be forced to come.' Bizelle intoned unhelpfully.

'Well, I'm glad you're here…we can catch up…make a night of it…what do you think?'

Bizelle lifted the glass in her right hand to her mouth and downed it carefully before answering. 'I am going to drink as many as these fluorescent yellow nasty things as I can humanly manage and whether you are standing in my vicinity or not makes *very* little difference to me.'

Tuula was shocked but not entirely surprised, they had never become well acquainted despite being thrown together on many occasions, but formerly they had always kept things light and pleasant; polite without ever wanting to go deeper than mere chit-chat. She knew Bizelle drank more than she should and weighed less than she ought, through mere observation, but she wondered what things had conspired to give her such an ugly outlook on life. 'Are you so unhappy?' She stopped, seeing Bizelle roll her eyes at the sympathy, realising too late that she may have come off sounding patronising. '- No, don't answer that. I'll join you on the yellows: there are places I'd rather be as well, so we might as well be miserable together.'

Tuula glanced over at her mother and Dune, now accompanied by Assinia, recently divorced from Kerq who was her father's FD. They were no doubt bitching about the men in their lives. Saphia caught her daughter's gaze and smiled, content to see her only child mingling in the crowd.

Tuula was satisfied that her mother had clocked her doing the social bit while she still had enough mental faculties to do so. It didn't take too long in that particular female crowd for her mother's few remaining rational brain cells to be switched off with the alcohol.

Tuula jerked her head in the direction of the front doors, saying 'I just need a little trip to the AC.'

She picked up her bag and noticed Bizelle's sceptical look. Nobody took bags to the ACs in this place, every conceivable need was catered for. If you had a fancy to buy a house while sitting on the toilet, you wouldn't be entirely surprised to see a 3D holo of an estate agent appear wearing a fixed smile.

She headed for the front door and kept going without looking back.

The water dripped off the multiple level roofs above Tuula's head, making a wet symphony in the dark as they landed on various thicknesses and types of metal; the disposal lids, the dwellings built by the dispossessed, the lamp surrounds. Plink, lunk, plip-lop. Tuula pulled her coat tighter around her chest and held it so that none of the cold could sneak around her neck. She hurried towards the blue lights pulsing from the entrance of the nighthop ahead, heading straight for the ladies' AC once inside the door. She had perfected this change over the years, and was deft in removing her shiny black coat, black evening gown, and earrings. She released her hopping gear from the vacuum-pack bag she carried under her shoulder, a rubberised mesh top and sleek knee length trousers, both in iridescent green.

Outside the building a group of men huddled in fierce discussion.

'Do we have to take him in here?' Detective Inspector Fraser Moldonny asked of his cousin, eyeing 'The Blue' with a disparaging raise of an eyebrow. 'Do you not think Denny's a bit old for this nighthop stuff? I saw a rest-eat up the road with big squashy chairs and a fire in the corner, we could take him there instead. Whaddya think?' Fraser waited, hopefully. He was not averse to the odd hopping session, but entering this portal of cool with his back-of-beyond cousin and their pushing-fifty uncle was not his idea of a good time.

'It's his stag night, cous. We gotta show the ol' man a whalloping time! This might be his last night of pure fun!'

'I thought the whole point of marrying again was to make him happy?' Fraser asked, knowing he would lose the battle, but determined to win the war.

'Hey pa!' Den Junior shouted to a man leaning against the side of a pod a hundred metres away. 'It's over here!'

Fraser ran back to the water edge and half hauled Denny back to his son, and an odd assortment of his other friends. Anything was better than listening to those two conduct their hilly-billy conversation at the tops of their voices.

'Fine, we go in here, but if Denny gets an MI you can go on the pad with him to the hospital. My interphone chip always scrambles when I go on those things,' Fraser grumbled.

'That's nurthin', Den junior's mate Patee chipped in, 'My gran'pa, he lost his hearin' tryin' ta save money with an ol' 'plant and an even older interphone…I think it were the series I!' Patee paused to shriek his amusement, 'Darn near would ha' lost his sight too, but for me grammy upt' an' pulled it out afore it were too late!'

Fraser seriously doubted the truth of this story. Certainly the first tests of inter-phones with auricular and orbital 'plants on *mice* had resulted in some loss of hearing and blindness before the techniques were perfected, and certainly there were some criminal groups who were still trying to perfect their own messy surgeries performed in all the splendour of a pod tower or a warehouse, but he'd never heard of a regular op going wrong in the last hundred years, nor did he think that trying to pull a chip out through the skin would be the way to rectify the problem! Surely these people weren't gullible enough to believe this pile of –

'Hey Patee! Does he still have the hole in his head?' One of the random older guys asked.

Fraser felt like banging his head against the wall; they were inside the sanctum of the Blue, and he was stuck with the least cool guys on Europa.

'How did you get tickets to this place, Den?' Fraser suddenly thought to ask. 'I've never even heard of anyone who didn't get blackballed at the door.'

'Probably best you jus' don' ask me cous.' Den Junior

replied with a wide grin, 'You bein' law enforcement an' all!' Fraser watched his cousin leer at a skinny blonde on the free-flow floor who raised an "I-am-way-out-of-your-league" eyebrow, and spun off to the other side of the anti-grav. unit. Fraser shook his head in despair and caught sight of a face smiling at him. It was a pale face, quite angular and slim with an expression in her eyes, and a poise that reminded him of a robin, willing to be friendly but ready to flee. How much had she heard? Would he have to explain all his relations or could he disown them completely?

'Nice mover.' She said, jerking her head towards Den Jnr, and smiling.

'I was just wondering whether I could get away with whisking you to the bar for a drink and disowning the sorry lot I came in with, but I guess not.' He paused, assessing her body language, and carried on, 'but how about I just do the whisking part instead?'

Tuula liked the way this guy gave her a sort of half smile, encouraging her to make the decision he wanted but not so arrogant that it put her off. She liked the way he wore his clothes just a little relaxed, like he made the clothes, not the clothes made him. She liked the way he was different from the other guys she knew, not so polished or so boring, there was a warmth in his eyes that hinted at real honest living; a modern day rogue in the twinkle town of New Manhattan. She wondered who would have taken the bribe to give them tickets. 'Whisk away,' she answered with a demure smile.

'So, I didn't catch your name?' Fraser asked, passing his wrist over the sensor and reaching for a drink beyond it with one smooth movement.

'I never threw it,' Tuula laughed at the unsubtlety, 'it's Tuula.' She took the drink he offered and sipped it, suddenly nervous she might have upset him.

'So,' Fraser started again in the same way, smiling, 'what do you do, Tuula?'

She normally hated it when people used her first name in a sentence, like a salesperson, but he made it sound like it was all part of the big game of chatting her up. She decided to play along, 'I'm looking…for the right job, I mean. I'm in the business of avoiding my family's business at the moment. I'm actually interested in aquaculturalism, that's what I've studied for.'

'Hmm.' Fraser nodded his head several times and held the interested and knowledgeable expression for a second, then caved in, 'so you want to be a sea farmer?' he grinned.

'Not the diver's suit, wellies, hands-on type farmer! The planning-crops, managing-water-areas, calculating-solar-energy type *aquaculturalist*!'

'And where would your nearest *water area* be then?' Fraser knew he was teasing, but hoped he had put enough warmth into his tone not to come across as scathing.

'Well, there's the problem.' Tuula spread her hands upwards in annoyance, warming to her favourite theme, 'Earth's waters are over-farmed, over-polluted, and who in their right mind would want to work there anyway…and the Domes don't make room for seas.'

Fraser thought he detected a note of censure towards the dome planners. 'Yep, people tend to want to live on dry land, it's true.'

Tuula continued regardless of his mockery, 'But that's just it! We have enough water in the dome because you need it for the weather cycle, but they just didn't think it out properly. So what I'm left with is the space tank option, which needs a lot of money…and now I'm back to the family business issue! Everything comes down to money, no matter how much you wish it didn't.'

'I guess, but I'd say everything comes down to money and morals, and the clash between the two.' Fraser thought briefly of his last case, and as quickly wiped it from his mind…talking to a pretty girl in a nighthop in the coolest town on Europa would need all his attention.

'Now what can you do, that would make you so wise to the human race?' Tuula asked, wanting to lead the conversation away from her for a while.

Fraser smiled; how would this affluent scrap of a girl react to his lowly profession? 'Lawman' he replied, thinking it can't be much different to a farmer, no matter what fancy name she gives it, or how rich her parents might be.

'You catch any bad guys lately?' She asked, inwardly cringing against such a corny line.

'A good shake less than I wish I'd caught, I – excuse me a minute,' the emergency tone caught Fraser's attention, he tapped his 'plant and a shaky holo appeared in front of him.

'DI Moldonny, the grid indicates you are the closest officer available to a robbery possibly taking place at this moment in Nollorton House – as in just down the street from where you are, Moldonny. Are you available, or shall I 'pad someone over there? We'd lose half an hour at least, and the fees to transport, but if you really can't do it, Ciegham's nearest after you.' The grey-haired holo narrowed his eyes, knowing he had scored a hit. He knew Ciegham was the sloppiest lawman around and several complaints had reached his desk already from other officers whose work was made twice as hard because of his inadequacies.

'As much as I'd like to get Ciegham out of his PJs this early in the morning, Sir, I'll go. ETA 2 minutes.' Fraser frowned, he couldn't have found a better way to ruin the best part of his night so far.

'If you run, your ETA would be 1 minute! Over and out.' The man chuckled as his holographic body flickered and disappeared.

Fraser glared at the space where his boss had been. He turned around, 'I'm sorry. I've gotta go, sharpish. Duty calls and all that.' Fraser winced in apology, he was unlikely to see this girl again any time soon.

Tuula took a big breath, 'Before you go, DI Moldonny, at least tell me your first name?'

Fraser grinned and started walking backwards 'Fraser, ma'am, at your service.'

Tuula thought if her heart was already in her mouth and her stomach flip-flopping between her feet and her throat, then his last cheeky wink would surely finish her off completely. She picked up her drink and sipped it, but strangely, the appeal of blue tingle lights, and freefall night hopping seemed to have lost its appeal. She felt strangely bereft standing at the bar. Not that it mattered. She would have to go home anyway. If there really had been a police emergency near here her parents might not stay around, and that meant she'd better be at home nursing some kind of illness, rather than admit she'd skipped a charity function for her own amusements.

Fraser jogged lightly down the dark street towards Nollerton House, sighing at the dismal truth that he was in fact running to the scene of the crime as his plaguey boss had suggested. He was guided by his 'plant's navigation, to save time finding the right house, but in fact he needn't have bothered, because the owners had installed a disturbingly gaudy name plate on their front wall, the letters of 'Nollerton' pulsing with the gleam of real flames.

The door man demanded ID, holding a portable scanner, and then abruptly changed to a more friendly (by doorman standards) tone when he read the device. 'Oh, Detective Moldonny, you certainly got here quickly. All the guests are in the function room. My employer, Ms Eastman, has reason to believe the perpetrator may still be in the building.'

'May I speak with her?' Fraser asked, quickly.

'Unfortunately not, however I know all the particulars. When she suspected there might still be an unlawful in the house she locked herself and all her guests in the function room until such a time as I could assure her it was dealt with.'

'How delightful.' Fraser responded, drily. 'Can you tell me why she supposes the guy is still in the house, and why she supposes that none of her guests could be our guy?'

'Yes sir, the safe has a timed access record, which shows entry at 6:00am, a mere minute before Ms Eastman happened to check it. Does seem odd, doesn't it, for it to be exactly on the hour? Regardless, as she initiated a lock down of her security immediately, we are assuming they are still somewhere in the building. Most of her guests tonight are old friends, I believe she has no reason to suspect anyone there of theft.'

'Hmm,' was all Fraser replied, 'can I see the safe? Do you know what items are missing?'

'If you'd like to follow me sir,' the doorman gestured up the broad staircase, 'there is only one item missing, but then there was only ever one item residing in it. The largest known Diamond, a vivid orange diamond to be exact, known as the "sunshine yellow". It was her most valuable possession, the last gift from her late husband.'

Fraser nodded his head. They passed down a gallery, through a smaller reception room, into a bedroom that looked so elegantly furnished and 'untouchable' that he couldn't be certain if the room was used or just for show. The safe was suspended in mid-air using some sort of energy field, and the door hung open. The edge of something shiny and white could be seen poking out. 'Can you lower it for – Hey!' Fraser called out, seeing a small figure drop past the window.

His legs were pounding down the corridor before his brain realised he was in hot pursuit. There were three doors on the left before he would reach the stairs, and he saw the third was open. His fingers pinched onto the door frame so that his momentum took him skidding around into the darkened room and he immediately felt a breeze from a window opening on to the rear of the property. His mouth set into a wide grimacing approximation of a smile with the effort of making the decision in the smallest amount of time possible, and having decided that this exit would be quicker but fervently wishing he was carrying his standard issue, he paused for just a second on the ledge to look at the gratifying vision of a slight figure beginning its escape from the garden. Probably heading for the east side quay – it would be easier to get lost over there away from the expensive housing. He would need to get the pods shut down, and soon. He vaulted diagonally down and sideways onto the top of a brick out-house and then leapt across to the top of the brick wall, allowing himself a fraction of a second for absolute satisfaction in his own unaided physical abilities, before running after the distant black suited figure. The guy was wearing bounders! He'd never catch him at this rate. Fraser tapped his implant to place a call for air assistance and remind them to shut down transport, forgetting that the action of bringing his left arm up, would move his centre of gravity slightly to the right. Not the ideal turn of events when you are running along the top of a two metre brick wall. He felt his foot slide off the corner and winced at the full length graze of skin meeting rough-edged hydrated silicate. His hand reached out to break his fall, but crumpled into the corner where the wall meets the ground, and then his body fell on top of it, but there wasn't time to register that particular pain before his head jarred on the ground with a sickening crack. His vision narrowed to two tunnels surrounded by darkness, and the world felt dizzy around him. Into one of the tunnels swam a black ovoid, making strange noises, two fingers felt his neck, and he wondered in a detached kind of way, whether he would die from strangulation. The last thing he saw before the tunnels completely closed in, was a flashing red light originating from something out of his line of sight.

* * *

That morning Ymarise Launay had kissed her son on the

cheek despite his squirming away, and watched as he found his seat on the school pod before moving to the 207 quay. She stared out of the window for most of the journey, dreaming of open spaces, and blocking out the shunting, grunting, powerful noises of the city.

As the pod slushed to a stop at the university's wharf, she breathed a sigh of relief at the formal gardens and buffalo grass lawns that they had fought to hold on to for so long, despite many generous offers on the land. She crossed the front lawn at an angle thereby entering through a less impressive side door. She experienced the small thrill of knowing her workplace well enough to walk all the back routes, and felt as though she really did fit in. She smiled at the power frame crew, busy at the ceiling of the first floor, and waved at Moss Saxon, coming up the main stairs, almost to prove her point to herself. She turned left, right, across a suspended corridor and down the hydrolift before passing her wrist over the chip reader at the entrance to the Applied Modern Physics block.

Ymarise fell into her chair, straining the old-style suspension, and exhaled, training her mind to today's tasks, and wiping all her household worries from her mind; they would all be waiting for her at 17:00, sure as space. Her class this morning was a small group of seven lads, three of whom she knew were squashed into Dave Gravestock's two-bed flat, in order to study here. They had a friendly camaraderie going, born of living in close proximity, which she'd found she could use to her benefit when teaching. They were currently two seminars in to the history of physics topic, and today's session was qubit teleportation of the 21st century.

She ran her fingers over her hub until she found the sensor switch to power it up, preferring to use good old-fashioned methods rather than remote thought commands. The display screen flickered into life in her left visual field, and as always she shifted backwards with her eyes closed to feel the back of her chair and then opened them again. She had inherited vertigo from her mother, but had still decided to have a 'plant and live with the occasional discomforts caused by her brain not coping well with two sets of visual information. She loaded her lesson up to the hub, and waited for the first 3D image of her presentation to appear. '*PAUSE*' she subvocalised her command to the hub.

Dave Gravestock and his cronies Guin Fenwick and Therg VonThering were the last to arrive, scuttling in at a lazy jog, and sliding in to their work stations.

'Inter-phones switched off please – emergency receives only,' Ymarise put a finger up to her left temple to do the same, and smiled expectantly to show she was ready to start.

They whizzed through 21st century knowledge of physics in three hours flat, covering superstring theory, bosons, gluons, gravitons and photons as they were then understood. She kept it light, never missing the opportunity to ridicule previous theories to make her students see the funny side to what could be a boring subject. She knew they would all want to listen though: Therg was interested in the teleportation industry, so would need to know all the history of the basics, and the others she suspected would be listening intently as they were close to earning the required knowledge credits to log onto the restricted interplanetary university lectures on the grid. She didn't take it to heart that she was a poor second to the lead scientists that featured on the grid. She would spend more time listening to Eär Omonv's current theories if she could…no, she corrected herself hastily, she would never regret her dedication to her family over her career. She was happy. People made their own happiness, that's what she believed.

'So,' she concluded, 'I would like a short 2000 word exposé on what you believe inhibited the 21st century physicists from discovering the true unified theory. I would like you to pay respect to how close some of them came, in what manner they erred and which details were later proved correct.' She paused to let that settle in, then continued: 'think about the ways in which they strove for truth: the search for smaller and smaller particles, and consider, if you think your word limit will allow it, the effect of religion versus science, and how this may have clouded their judgement.

Dave willed his view of the lecture to fade so it was nearly transparent, and saved it as 'Exposé 3', to be downloaded to his hub when they got back to his digs. He flipped his inter-phone back to 'receive all' mode and lifted his eyes to Therg.

'*YOU READY?*' he sent to Therg's code.

'*YEP*' Therg subvocalised, adding Guin's code to make a three way link, '*I'M READY, DO WE NEED ANYTHING ON THE WAY BACK?*'

Therg cut the connection as the other two came to stand next to him, 'We don't have any seminars this afternoon do we?'

'Nope, nothing til tomorrow, 14:00' Guin answered.

Dave sighed, 'then my friends, we are definitely going to need some supplies. There was nothing for brekkie this morning except seaweed pickle and tinned cham. Needless to say, I am ravenous.'

'Therg, my man, has your grant from your Dad's company materialised yet?' Dave asked, aware that the rent he was owed would pay for this shopping trip nicely.

'Hang on, I'll just check my funds on the grid, hang on a sec,' Therg tapped his 'plant and frowned a little in concentration. He had a long face with a large bone structure and dark, fine hair. His family had old Earth Russian and Scottish origins but he had grown up on Lunar 13. Therg frequently boasted that LPD 13 had forced the last of the numerical superstitions to come to an end last century. Unlike LPDs 4, 5, 8 and 11 which had been assigned a mortifying alternate use, LPD 13 had thrived. Politicians and citizens alike involved with failed domes seemed to lose either money or reputation to such a degree that it ruined their lives. Some had even lost their lives when poor or frustrated societies turned malevolent on each other. But lunar 13 had not failed, it had succeeded to the point where its democratic, affluent society was more sought after than 17, and powerful families with important industries on 13, were able to increase their profits and market elsewhere. Therg was the third son of the Von Therings, often called the McThergs, by Dave - to his own vast amusement - and while he was well-off in theory, his family had a laid-back attitude to funds that only the rich can fully understand. He had been sent to 17 to learn the family trade of transportation, and hopefully bring back some insight into cornering the growing market over there for personal use telepads.

'I got them. I'm nearly as affluent as Eär Omonv's first wife after settlement.' His deep set eyes crinkled, but the smile didn't spread. He liked his humour dry.

'Right then Dave, it's celebration time. Time to buy some bog roll!' Guin remarked jovially. His parents lived in New Aberystwyth at the far edge of the dome, a mere 50 kilometres away, but they had taken longer as a town to buy all the latest technologies, therefore telepadding was not an option, and the pods, while ecologically very valuable, were slow in comparison to the golden era of the oil reserves on old Earth, before the migrations and de-teching of the 22nd century. So it was that Guin was grateful to kip on the floor of Dave's flat during the week, and Therg was either too well-mannered or too laid-back to mind.

The three young men entered their flat on the 9th floor and fell through the door, dropping essential supplies on the dusty carpet as they proceeded to the small kitchen. There were bottles, sachets and packets waiting to be recycled littering most of the floor in the living area. The dust threatened to rise up the bases of the three chairs like a primordial being seeking a place to slob out. One corner of the living space housed a messy collection of monitoring equipment, portable accelerators and mini teleportation devices in bits, all resting on a surface improvised between two chests that Dave had originally used to move his meagre possessions when his Great Grandad had left him the flat in his will. Most of the available light was taken up by Therg's prize and joy on the window sill – a tub for his turnips, and a tank designed to simulate growing conditions in the ocean off Siberia. The tub, being round, was almost falling off the thin shelf while the tank made it bow in the middle. Therg went immediately to croon loving words to his disease-killing super seaweed and his all-season turnips, 'Good afternoon, my pretties. How are we today? Tundra? Tilly? Tallulah? Would you care for some phosphorous enriched phytofood?'

'Tallulah Turnip?' Guin exclaimed laughing, 'You know

you are a complete nutjob, Therg of the McThergs!'

'Von Thering, not McTherg, you Celtic pony. He laughs now, Tilly, but when he feasts on my smoked turnip, he'll soon change his mind.' Therg's tones were reverent.

Guin bent down to pick up the littered shopping on the carpet and grabbed a bit of fluff as he did so. 'Will you look at this by yer, lads? We have *got* to do some tidyin' today, if it's the last thing we do.'

Dave grinned at Therg, knowing which of the three of them reached their dirt intolerance level first.

Guin could be heard muttering as he tidied take-eat containers to the overflowing rubbish bag 'Ah, Nora Jones, boys, what's goin' on with this…I swear if I died my body would rot on that carpet before you even moved me…probably trip over my liquefying head, break your flaming ankle most likely…wouldn't be surprised if you couldn't even be bothered to get it fixed…probably get gangrene in your fingers…I'd probably spent my afterlife staring at your disease-ridden green fingers, you ponies.'

* * *

'Wuurgh?' Fraser croaked.

'My friend, easy, relax.' The soft lilting accent of his partner cleared some of the fog in his brain.

Fraser cleared his voice and tried again, 'Varn? Where am I?'

'In hospital, and lucky to have your jelly head that will cope with a little clash with the floor from time to time! Pity your arm is not so soft! Compound fracture my friend, and two days of rest, bien sur.'

Fraser looked down at his lurid green polymorph cast covering his left hand and arm. 'I take it I'm back on Lunar 17?'

'Bah, yes! No expense spared for the brave young lawman flinging himself out of houses to catch the wicked villains!' Varn Delot leaned back in his chair and chuckled. He had a lean wiry frame, was older than Fraser by about ten years and had the kind of skull that suits very short hair. The grey hair, he always quipped, would stop at nothing less than complete domination of his head. So far, the brown was holding its own.

'Villain, not villains. Small, too. I suppose it could have been a girl.' Fraser looked at Varn to see how he reacted to this piece of news.

'Bah…' Varn was the King of non-committal noises. 'They found bounders at East Side. Size 42. Could be girl, could be boy.'

'East Side! I knew it! What about the vertical running I saw? What equipment did they have for that?'

'Four dents in ground, they left nothing other at the house.'

'Hmm, expensive kit then. I can't believe I won't get to follow this one up. I saw them for space's sake!' Fraser stopped suddenly, remembering more detail of the night before and picturing the red flashing light, 'Say, how did you guys find me? Do I remember a beacon lying next to me or am I dreaming it?'

'Interesting aspect, certainement. Psyche profile for an unlawful who takes time to dial a recovery team. Whoever takes on the case will 'ave much to look at *here*.' Varn had to put in extra effort to squeeze out an 'h', despite over ten years speaking English.

'I've got to get up! Maybe I can convince the boss to let me liaise with Europa?' Fraser started picking off the stickers that monitored breathing, heart rate and so on routinely, and swung his feet round onto the floor. He felt a curious rush of blood round his eyes then a draining of blood from his face, 'Jeez, what painkillers did they give me, I feel worse than crap.' He sunk back on the pillows and took a steadying breath.

'Is your jelly head I suspect,' Varn replied easily, lifting his eyebrows slightly, 'I suggest you find a bit of skin with some blood still under it, to stick your monitors onto before you 'ave half the hospital in 'ere.'

Sure enough a junior grade nurse appeared with her eyes rolling as if patients that removed their stickers were the bane of her life, despite most of them being twice her age. She deftly replaced the important three. 'Nice to see you with us again Mr Moldonny…do try not to move again just yet – you only came out of critical an hour ago, we're working on your CSF and ionic balance you know, shouldn't be more than half an hour before you're feeling right again.' She tapped a few things into the computer bank controlling his monitors, drips and so on behind his bed, and left.

'Patronising little upstart, scrawny, good for nothing kid.' Fraser grumped, rubbing his hand across his eyebrows.

'If it will keep you 'appy enough to stay in your bed I 'ave some other news for you.'

'Yeah?' Fraser sighed, he doubted any news would subdue the pounding in his head.

'They found a calling card.'

'A what?'

'Is an old, bah... *thing*, it means they leave name at scene of crime.'

'What? Like a pseudonym? Sounds theatrical. How does that cheer me up exactly?'

'Written on a white plate in the vault was "the interplanetary dinner set gang"; it points to more than one person, no?'

'Yeah, maybe a whole group of them, but why are you telling me this when we won't be on the case?'

'*Interplanetary* no? Who got the interplanetary liaison officer promotion this year, ah?'

'You think I could argue they *will* have multiple *and* interlunar crimes from just a name?'

'I think it is your best shot, my friend.' Varn tapped his 'plant and brought up the news cast. He sat absorbed in the monotonous drone for several minutes.

Fraser glanced down at his arm, firmly encased in the green polymorph cast. 'I've just thought,' he directed at an unresponsive Varn, but being used to ploughing through seemingly impenetrable silences, he continued regardless, 'if I'm back on Lunar 17 my 'plant will have crashed again...it never survives the padding – must be a glitch, I'll have to download all my codes again from my hub,' he paused to give Varn ample opportunity for a grunt, but the man was absorbed, 'so if you try to call me I won't know who you are okay?'

'Hnng' Varn replied.

'So the boy, or man, or whatever...' Fraser started summarising idly.

'Such finesse my friend. When was the last time you even spoke to a whatever? They have a name you know, most people call them women.'

'Ah, welcome back – interesting article was it?' Fraser remarked drily. 'As it happens, I spoke to a very nice whatever last night. Outclassed me though!' Fraser grinned, reminiscing about a pair of laughing eyes. She was worth the inferiority complex.

'Vraiment? But who outclasses a lawman?' Varn smiled lazily.

'How about the daughter of a business mogul from Europa, seemingly quite at home in 'The Blue' in New Manhattan?' Fraser asked with a resigned expression.

'Hm Mm. That would do it my friend,' Varn agreed.

'So what about this Boy/Man/Whatever? Ha, BMW, we should call them that! How you planning on catching 'eem?'

'What's with the 'you', Varn? Are you planning a vacation?'

'Baaah, but don't I always look to my smart young partner for all my important decisions?' Varn smiled with his eyes and then closed them, feigning a snooze, 'these old bones get tired, my friend, you figure out how to catch your villains and I will recharge 'ere for a while.'

'Just because I have a drip in my arm doesn't mean I couldn't kick your ass.' Fraser replied matter-of-factly.

Varn opened one eye slowly. 'Yes, no doubt. Who wouldn't be afraid of the zero-G lawman?'

'Nothing wrong with a good solid zero-G grappling hook. Can't go wrong with one of those on your belt. This new technology can't replace good craftsmanship. I'll not have a word said against it!'

Varn mouthed the words along with Fraser, as if he had heard them before.

'And don't think I don't know what you're doing!' Fraser added indignantly.

The newspaper screen bobbed up and down as silent chuckles rocked through Varn's ample chest, to the point where he gave up reading. 'You know they laugh at me, for having so old-fashioned a partner.'

'Not as much as they laugh at me for having such an old timer as you are for a partner!' Fraser smiled limply from his pale face.

Varn brought his hands to his chest, 'Yet again I am mortally wounded by one I had thought was my true friend.

Alas, I fear my old head must rest now, such a busy day as I 'ave 'ad…' Varn paused and closed his eyes. '…running down 'ere…re-organising your day…' he opened one eye, with a twinkle, '…fending off all kinds of female nurses wanting to wash your ass…'

'Uurgh, my head.' Fraser resorted to being ill again, 'Hey, I just remembered, all my equipment zoned out when I got close to the unlawful…it's gotta be expensive gear to interfere with my power.

'Kaiza Kent is out of prison.' Varn murmured.

'Who? I don't even know the name.' Fraser frowned.

'The guy who embezzled all the money from Mars Dome Company during the evacuation. Not that it mattered much in the end…Mars was always going to be bankrupt, but 'e was still put away.'

'Must have been before my time.' Fraser just managed to keep the smile out of his voice.

'I don't understand why no-one seems to succeed on Mars.' Varn tapped his screen away completely, prepared for once to chat, 'It 'as too much bad publicity, while Lunar Ventures seems to do no wrong…I do not trust such good fortune my friend. It seems to me, if it looks too good to be true, they will most certainly be 'iding something.'

'It wasn't just bad publicity, as I recall. It was bad shielding.' Fraser shuddered. 'You can't expect people to live in Domes without a sense of security above them.'

'I still say people seem to 'ave confidence in lunar communities for no good reason.'

'What I need,' began Fraser, dragging the conversation back to what interested him the most, 'is clearance to all the old internet archives to look up 'calling cards' and any links to old crimes.'

'What you need,' sighed Varn, with emphasis, 'is clearance from the boss to get started on this case.'

'Ah, but you forget, my fine partner…the boss owes me one for my swift response yesterday on my night off!'

'Hmmng.'

3 SEVERANCE

If the famous Gallic grunt had indeed been doubting of a positive outcome, Fraser could now smile in smug satisfaction as he stepped on to the cushion of air in the archive section of the library and observed the images rushing past him as he approximated walking through the internet archives. He was exasperated to think that his 'plant would not interface with so old a system, when it linked seamlessly to the grid. Instead, the images were generated by the specially designed room in the library.

He 'walked' through a door labelled twentieth century crimes, and saw several options before him: 1900 – 1920, 1921 – 1940, 1941 – 1960, 1961 – 1980, and so on with detailed subheadings. A phrase caught his eye: 'the rise of the jewel thieves'. He tried to activate the heading subvocally, and then remembered he was in the library, he then tried vocally with several old commands that he knew of, and finally remembered he had been issued with a glove, and reached up to touch the 1961 – 1980 section. He grumbled about the system, thinking it was used more as a museum to attract tourists than as a true representation of the technology back then. Surely nobody would use a system so reliant on repetitive movements.

The first entry was for Doris Payne, a seventy year old small time jewel thief, not vastly different to a regular shoplifter, with reminiscences from security guards who knew her well. The other entries yielded nothing better and he wasted twenty minutes looking through them, hoping that thoroughness would give him his just rewards. After that he looked up the definition of 'calling card', and then cross referenced them together. This brought up an entry or 'Web page' as he was supposed to call it, which made him feel a kick of adrenaline. "The dinner set gang (aka The Fat Cat Burglars)" it read, "was a gang of thieves who became notorious in the late 1960s and 1970s for their burglaries of the homes of the wealthiest Americans while the victims were at home eating dinner. Newspapers in New York City and Florida nicknamed them The Dinner Set Gang."

Fraser read on, noting the names of the group, their mode of operation and their notoriety. He couldn't help the flood of questions it evoked; could the new gang be direct descendants, would they also target the wealthy, would their psyche profile tend in the same direction as their namesakes, would he be able to justify interviewing his rich robin? He grinned, probably not.

As he left the archive room he asked for a download of that chunk of data, and five minutes later was handed a flat text copy. The attendant apologised for the printing time, and Fraser tried to keep the look of disgust off his face for the lack of a decent data chip.

A gilt-edged invitation was personally delivered to Fraser's apartment that afternoon. It sped up the mail shoot and drifted for a second in mid-air, before following a series of swooping zigzags to the mock oak poly floor. Inside the cream envelope glistened a microfine slice of gold weaved next to the same of aquamarine. Its art deco font would describe to its privileged reader a ball of stunning magnificence on Enceladus. Fraser sloped up the stairs, swung through the door and pulled a section of the floor up into a chair shape; making an espresso while he waited for this evening's furniture to set. He opened the stiff cream envelope, feeling its expense on his rough fingertips, and wondered who Mr & Mrs Saussay were. A handwritten note fell from behind the invite and Fraser caught it midway to the floor. 'Dear Fraser,' it began, 'my wife Saphia and I are acquainted with the personal commitment and evident progress already made in the matter of apprehending the felon who has so upset Mariposa Eastman's household recently. In recognition of our appreciation of your diligence I hope you will appreciate a small gesture from me in the shape of an invitation to a forthcoming event, namely…' Fraser stopped reading, a puzzled frown crinkling one side of his forehead more than the other. He tapped his plant, subvocalised a query to the grid, and brought up a file outlining Herve Saussay's latest business acquisitions, his main interests seemed to be on Enceladus but Europa also kept coming up as he scanned the text. Why would some random guest at Mrs Eastman's house offer him some kind of doggy treat for doing his job? He queried "Saussay family" and mentally clicked on an article written for Money Week entitled 'The private life of Herve Saussay'. He scanned down until he found the name he had been hoping for… 'Tuula Saussay, the only daughter of Europa's favourite tycoon, might be this year's biggest marital catch but she has no idea of marrying yet awhile. Giles Brandforth, heir to the Brandforth Hotels Syndicate, no stranger to Tuula's personal habits and tastes, told us exclusively that she has no plans to wed.'

Fraser tapped his plant without bothering to close the file and then rubbed the spot he had hit harder than he realised. So he knew her name, and all his original suppositions were correct. Had she been responsible for the cream envelope he was still gripping? He relaxed his grip and took satisfaction in scrumpling it into a ball and chucking in a practised manner towards the spot on his wall which would flip open to access the garbage shoot. The missile missed its target area and bounced once on the floor before coming to an abrupt stop.

*   *   *

Tad drifted in and out of consciousness for two hours after the strong painkillers were injected. He registered wisps of conversation that all seemed to merge together alarmingly. 'Look at that, they've stuck the matched bone spray to his arm for safe keeping – it's all tangled in his hairs…no, leave him there, he's on his way to the ward… Can I stay with him? Yes, although he won't be much company for you'… A pink wall, his mother's face, a strange Irish voice, a pencil on a table – no sense waking up yet…no-one seems to be here, 'Where's dad?'(Was that his own voice?) – 'he'll be on the next transport, you go on back to sleep now'.

'Mum?' Tad blinked in the darkness.

'Yes! I'm here. It's ok.'

'I suppose they finished the trip without me.'

'Yes, sweetheart, it's eighteen hundred, do you want the

light on?'

Tad let out a breath, 'No thanks…Is Dad here?'

'He was here for an hour. I sent him back to get some food. We can go home after your next observation.'

'I'm tired.' Tad proved it by letting out a yawn.

'I'm going to take the day off tomorrow so your leg can heal.' Ymarise yawned behind her hand, not wishing her son to see how tired she was feeling. It was probably just the inactivity. That, and the stifling heat in hospitals.

A nurse came to the end of the bed and tapped the screen embedded into the foot of his bed. She was wearing a name badge with a glittery star sticker on it, and she had two styluses and a pair of scissors sticking out of her pocket.

'So, you're awake now!' It was the Irish voice from before. The voice was also overly bright, and Tad suddenly felt too old to be on a paediatric ward. 'Well now, I think that's all in order. I'll get you some analgesies, and then you can be off home with your mam. How's that?'

Ymarise leapt in, 'That will be great, thank you. Won't it Tad?' She looked at her son expectantly, and raised both eyebrows for a fraction of a second.

'Yes.' He lifted his leg out from under the duvet and felt the additional weight of the polymorph cast. 'Pink?' he cried out in revolted distress.

'Oh I know,' the Irish-voiced lady began to explain, 'the last green one was snapped up by a lovely young lawman just before you in the casting room, and I know you won't begrudge him it when he was injured in the line of duty, so to speak. We are due a pad delivery any hour now, but for the moment, everyone is in pink. Now, it will only be on for a day or so, so there'll be nothing to worry about!'

*   *   *

'Nothing to worry about! Yes, I'm sure you *would* think that, you stupid... Irish... selfish witch!' Tad muttered, blinking back the tears two days later as he washed the words Pinky Stinky off his locker. Frel and he had been joking about his stupid girl's cast and it had been fine. It had been their own private joke, but somehow the other boys had joined in, and every day it seemed that he was doing less of the laughing, and more of the being laughed at. Still, Frel had stuck by him, nothing would change that. He had even helped Tad pick the pink cotton wool out of his science experiment, and thrown the pink candy apple placed in his lunchbox in the bin. Not that he cared what anyone did to him anyway. They were just stupid boys. He was going to be rich. His Daddy always told him how he would be the star of the family. He was going to ace school and earn tons of credit and hire Authex Ancors as his own personal AC cleaner.

*   *   *

Edytha pulled up the waistband of her trousers and wondered why she bothered trying to lose weight when her husband never noticed when she finally managed it. Not that he'd be slow to point out to her if her trousers got tight. Always the rod with him and never the carrot. What a donkey he made of her! She sighed, hoisted the lid of her propagation tank back in place and carried a trug full of seedlings that needed potting out, back to the kitchen.

'Don't tell me I can't bring them in here Oszkár, I know you don't like it, but I promise you there is nowhere else to do it, and no matter what you say that shed isn't big enough. I can't swing bat or cat in that hole.' Edytha plonked the trug on the table in a shower of soil.

'Fine, don't talk to me then, but if you will be in bad mood for rest of day I would sooner know it now.' She ignored looking in his corner of the room to avoid eye contact, not wanting to be the first to give in.

'No doubt you will like tubers when they are put in front of you and *then* there will be no complaining, eh?' Edytha kicked the door open with more violence than was necessary. Not talk to me will he? She stomped across the yard, picked up a sack of super Kwik-Grow compost and brought herself noisily back into the kitchen.

She fixed her husband with a scowl and seeing him, dropped the compost all over the floor. Her stomach rushed up to meet her throat, and the room seemed to drop away to either side of her as she reached her husband's chair, clasped his pale, stiff hand and whispered his name, knowing with growing panic, that she would never hear him reply.

She reached up to tap her plant and subvocalised the emergency code. A holographic image projected in front of her: 'Law or Life?' came the clinical response. Oskar and she had always joked about the emergency code, particularly when they were young, and the galaxy was literally in front of them. How many times had they stolen a kiss over a dead body? She shuddered and cried and rocked, trying to stop the cold sweat carrying her into a faint, clasping her hand over her mouth in disbelief… the problem was it was never meant to be her husband's body. Tears rolled down her face unchecked. The grief formed an iron ball in her throat, but refused to release. The pleasant-faced lady recording tried again, 'I'm sorry, please restate: law or life?'

'Life' Edytha replied in a dead voice. A new face appeared, this time with a real human behind it. 'Hello, are you injured?'

'It's my husband.' Edytha answered, still not believing it could be.

*   *   *

Tad ran effortlessly towards Frel, glad there was no hint of a limp that might remind his classmates of any of the not so funny names they had invented for him since the pink cast had become common knowledge. 'Hey! Frel! Wait up!'

He walked next to his friend, gathering his breath to tell him the exciting news. 'Have you seen the new Stone jackets in 'Milo's'?' he gasped out before his lungs had calmed down.

'What's stone?' Frel asked, bending down to inspect a scuff on his shorts, and getting side-tracked by a scab on his ankle.

'Stone – you know, the one that flares up in sync with your footsteps, the one where it changes pattern and when you walk next to someone with the same label, you can glow in time to each other, and have images moving from one jacket to the other!

'Yeah, I remember,' Frel instantly invented, 'I read it in...you know.'

Tad was not listening, he was reeling off the prices of each jacket, how many boys were likely to be able to afford them, and wondering whether he might get one as a birthday present. 'And how smack would that be, if you got one too, we could share all our images and it would be – you just made that scab bleed.'

Frel picked it off completely, 'Yeah I know.' He inspected it closely and then thrust it to within an inch of Tad's nose. 'Look at that!'

Tad's head jumped back and his body followed, 'That is gross and putrid and sick. Get rid of it.' He held out an imaginary shield with his hand until the scab was safely flicked into the grass.

'I'd have Mirianda Lacklonne on mine.' Frel mused.

'Eh?' Tad brought his friend back into focus, having been staring at the progress of an ant over the cracked mud and grass.

'The Stones...I'd have Mirianda on mine.' Frel grinned and his friend grinned back. Mirianda Lacklonne needed no further explanation. 'You know what I'd really like though, although I'm never gonna get it...the new Telepath [III], the A2G4 with the high res. holo's for face to face, and the new subvocal clarity 'ware for private chat.'

'Is that the one with the grid interface so that two people

can experience the same portion of the grid as if they were side by side?' Tad asked, quoting specifications as easily as Frel.

'Yep! It's sub-cool. I can't get it anyway. I'm not allowed an upgrade until I'm eighteen.'

'No, me neither. And even if I got it done without them knowing I couldn't afford the surgery.'

'Yeah.' Frel sighed. They lapsed into the silence of unattainable dreams.

'Oh, crap-in-the-hole. Look who it is.' Tad controlled the full body shudder with difficulty at seeing Mesril. He was the ring leader of the boys. Tad wasn't sure whether anyone actually liked him, but he was certainly feared. If you didn't want your most embarrassing memories continually plastered across the collective consciousness of the school, then you didn't cross him.

'Just don't look,' said Frel, looking. 'He's coming over.'

Tad kicked the floor with one foot, affecting nonchalance at the expense of his already scuffed shoe.

'Hey Tadelesh.' Mes drew out his name with menacing intent.

Tad raised his eyebrows, not trusting his voice.

Mesril felt the fear nevertheless. It was irresistible. 'You wearing pink pants today Tad?' There was a scattering of suppressed giggles.

'I don't know, are you?' Tad tried the sarcastic approach.

'Has mummy put a pink hanky in your pocket today Tad? I'm surprised she let you outside all on your own!' Mesril, worked up to his grand finale. He took a theatrical glance at his watch. 'In fact, isn't it your bedtime, Tad?

Tad decided the time for sarcasm was long past. 'Why don't you just back off, Mes? Go pick on someone your own size, and by that I do mean FAT!' It was a bold bluff. Tad thought he would probably get a punch straight in the face for it. And right now he wouldn't mind waking up in hospital again just for this to be over.

Mes was only thrown for a second, 'At least I'm not a scrawny little runt like you!' He advanced a step. 'At least I don't wear pretty little pink socks, and pink little mittens.' He smiled an evil smile, back to familiar territory, and advanced another step.

'Fight, fight, fight!' Three of the four lads behind Mes, including Authex Ancors, Tad noticed, picked up the chant and he took a moment to grin at them.

Frel glanced up the road meaningfully. 'I think we passed a lawman just now – probably best not to start anything.'

Aaron Plesser was the only of Mesril's lot to look a little concerned. He wasn't chanting. 'Listen, Mes – he's right. It's stupid to do it here.'

'I'm not afraid to fight you!' Tad yelled, hoping they would back down with his pride still intact.

Frel widened his eyes meaningfully at Aaron, sensing an ally.

'Come on Mes, let's go check out the air park.' Aaron said,

earning a smile from Frel.

Mesril smiled and gave a parting shot. 'Wouldn't want to see your pink guts anyway.'

'Everyone's guts are pink.' Tad muttered, watching them walk away. 'That's probably going to make it worse now.' He turned to Frel. 'I wish Aaron had kept his big mouth shut. Then it would all be over now.'

'We were only trying to stop Mesril from mashing your face!' Frel grinned.

Tad couldn't think of anything except his best friend and one of his tormentors united by that one word 'we'. He grunted something unintelligible.

'What?' Frel asked.

'I said I'm going home,' Tad enunciated the last word with annoyance, 'You want to get something to eat at mine?'

Frel hesitated. 'No, I can't. I've got to get home too.'

Tad walked home, scudding the ground on every step. He remembered that his friend would walk past the air park on his way home. Frel wouldn't have to worry about it when he was on his own.

*   *   *

Edytha packed her lunch into a small blue cush-cell, as she had done every Wednesday when visiting the town for supplies; she caught pod 19B, and tried hard not to think of what her husband would have said as it wharfed with a soft slap of water. She walked quickly to the cemetery, being careful to keep her brain active with carefully posed thoughts inside her head such as 'What a nice haircut. Lovely fresh air. That is a big building, I wonder how many floors it has? Onetwothr-f-f-si-seven! Wow, seven floors.'

She entered through the impressive tall iron gates with flaking white paint, made her way to the fresh grave, arranged herself carefully on an antique fleece rug she had bought on Earth more than ten years ago, and all of a sudden her plans for the day finished.

She read the tombstone three times. Once normally, once to take in the exact meaning of each word and once more to make sure she hadn't missed any of it.

> **Oszkár Orlov**
> **2354 ~ 2437**
> **Steadfast husband to Edytha Orlov.**
> **May the earth be light upon you.**
> **Rest well; heed not our grieving.**

'You khazer! You momzer!' She whispered. The rustling of the trees answered her silently.

'Why did you have to leave me?' She dragged in a shaky breath, 'What am I supposed to do now?' Edytha cried for several minutes, until her throat hurt and her eyes felt too puffy to blink. There was nobody to see and she now felt too blank to continue.

'I suppose you would tell me off Oszkár.' She sighed, 'for being infernal ninny.'

'Why were you always grumbling at me, Oszkár? Were you so unhappy? Were you so unhappy that you had to leave me?' She felt the lump rise up again to her throat and forced it back down awkwardly with a difficult swallow.

'Did you think I didn't know? When you raised your eyes to heaven, or when you looked at me like I was worth nothing to you…did you think about how *I* might feel? Did you?'

Edytha walked about agitatedly for a minute or so before slumping back in front of the clean stone. 'No, I don't suppose you did,' she croaked, 'well, don't expect me to feel sorry for you because I don't! I DON'T, do you hear? I'm glad it was you and not me! I'm glad!'

Edytha wiped the back of her hand across her eyes several times, and ineffectually smeared the tears across her face. It didn't matter anyway. Nobody looked at her now. Nobody looked at her before either. Nothing changed.

4 INADEQUACY

'Daaaad?' Tadelesh asked with a loaded tone.

'Yeeees?' His father replied warily.

'Can I have a Stone jacket for my birthday?'

'What's that then m'boy?'

Tad rolled his eyes at the ineptitude of parents in general. 'It's only the smackest thing there ever was Dad! It's this new material that looks like stone and feels like stone but you can wear it like a jacket and it's got a surface woven electrophoretic display which I could link with Frel's if he got one too and –'

'Woah there, take a breath sunshine. You sound just like your mother when she gets going with physics. Remember your poor old Dad is just a simple gardener.'

Bracq grinned at his son and made an imbecilic face with crossed eyes and tongue sticking out of the side of his mouth. Since Tad knew this routine well, and knew his Dad was never serious about his work being more menial than his mother's, he hit him with an open fist, following through a little too violently when Bracq jumped sideways out of the way. 'Daaaaad.'

'What? Too slow for me? Are ya? Hey?' Since each word was punctuated by a poke in the ribs Tad was soon screaming with delight and running round the room, with a fresh scream every time the direction of running was changed.

When they both finally collapsed in a heap, Tad looked up into his Dad's reddened face and asked, 'So can I have a Stone jacket for my birthday then Dad?'

'Bracq laughed, 'You've got the memory of an elephant, m'boy. We'll see. Your birthday is still a while away, you might change your mind –'

'Oh Dad!'

'*And*,' Bracq continued doggedly, 'we'll have to see how much it is…and how good you've been…and how much your mother's earned!'

Ymarise walked into the room with her stern but kind face on, Tad knew it could only mean one thing. 'Bed time young man.'

'Up the stairs quick as you can, brush your teeth and then your mum will read you a story,' Bracq shouted up the stairs at the receding bottom of his eight year old: 'if you're good!'

'He's usually good when you're here,' Ymarise smiled, 'he dotes on you.'

Bracq shared a smile of parental pride. 'He is a good boy. Did you hear what he wants for his birthday?'

'Yes, and I know the price as well. We might manage it at a stretch. Have you got any overtime coming up?'

'Not really,' Bracq rubbed his bottom lip and widened his mouth into a calculating grimace, 'but I'll ask around at work. Is it your turn or mine for the story?'

'Yours, of course!' Ymarise smiled to take the sting out of it, 'It's not often he sees you at bedtime now with your new shift pattern.'

'Tell me about it!' Bracq sighed, 'And it will only get worse if I take on more for this present. It's a shame they don't pay you to do a bit extra.'

'I know, it's an all-inclusive wage. There's nothing I can do.' Ymarise knew this was a sore point. If she was allowed to do more for overtime credit she could earn the amount they needed in half the time, and her husband wouldn't have to miss so many bedtimes. She resolved to stop thinking about it though, because she knew from past experience that she would only get bitter. The truth was she didn't think Bracq saw her job as hard work, and the fact that she looked after Tad most of the time and he couldn't made him envious rather than sympathetic. She sought to change the topic of conversation, 'You know Tad got his first lowish grade the other day.'

'Oh yeah?'

'It was only for one subject, don't make a big deal about it, I think some of the boys have been giving him trouble since he broke his arm.' Ymarise wondered if she should have kept her mouth shut.

'Which subject?' Bracq asked, his tone hardening a little.

'Maths. But really, it was only a C-, and I'm sure he'll get it back up next term.'

'I'll talk to him.' Bracq held both hands up when he saw his wife's expression. 'I'll talk to him nicely… I promise.'

Ymarise shook her head with a smile on her face, hearing her husband tear up the stairs in much the same way that Tad had done just a few minutes ago.

Bracq dimmed the light in Tad's room and joined him on the bed, 'Do you know why I haven't got the job I always dreamed of?'

'You earn good credit Dad.' Tad said seriously.

'You are by far too young to be worrying about how much I earn. It's enough, that's all.'

Since Tad was aware exactly how much his Dad brought home after glancing at his wage FT, but was equally aware he probably shouldn't have seen it, he wisely kept quiet.

'Anyway,' Bracq continued, 'I want better for you. When I was a boy your age,' his voice dropped into storytelling mode and Tad snuggled his head onto Bracq's chest to listen to a well-rehearsed tale, 'I used to love Maths. It was my all-time favourite subject. When I'd been doing Maths for an hour I felt like I really understood the numbers, like they made up a big weaving that made sense from all angles, no matter how you wove them.' Bracq sighed and squeezed his son tight into his side, 'But then I got in with the wrong crowd and by the time I was fifteen I was leaving school and my future path through life was set right then. You can't wind back the years, much as you might want to, and you can never learn as much as you're doing right now. It's the best opportunity of your entire life, Tad. You won't waste it like your silly old Dad did, will you?' Tad snuggled deeper into his Dad's jumper and shook his head, but he was thinking 'No, Dad, I promise I won't.'

Bracq made the imbecile face, and Tad grinned, which made Bracq laugh so that his chest shook and wobbled Tad's head.

Ymarise popped her head around the door, 'Time for a bed time story?'

'Mum!' Tad craned his neck around to show her his face, 'I want the one about the lucky boy!'

Bracq laughed, 'And this is where I pass you over to your mother. All yours story queen!'

'Oh unfair!' Ymarise smiled and Tad smiled too without really knowing why.

'Dad wants to listen too, don't you Dad?'

'Yes Dad,' Ymarise imitated, 'you want to listen with your son don't you?'

Bracq leaned back against the wall, manoeuvring the head of a teddy to take the edge off the discomfort, 'Don't I just.'

'Once upon a time, there was a little boy called Tadelesh, who lived by the ancient river of Niger which has twisted through Mali for many centuries. Where it widens and slows down is a little village called Douentza and the Dogon people who lived there say that it slows down to bid them good day on its journey to the sea. Tadelesh slept on the roof of his earth house by night and caught Bushi fish by day which he sold at market every fifth day.

'The little boy Tadelesh was never unhappy. He had been blessed with luck. Every morning, when he awoke to the tickle of sunshine on his nose, he knew no worries. He knew that he just needed to trust in his GGP.'

'No mum, you said it wrong, you have to say it properly.' Tad murmured, churlish in his increasingly sleepy state.

Ymarise continued gently, 'He had to trust in his very own Greater Galactic Plan.'

Bracq raised an eyebrow at his wife – he was fairly sure she had added her own religious beliefs to the original story. He mentally corrected himself; how many times had she told him it was not a religion? It was merely a way for rational and scientific minds to come together and rejoice in their spirituality, without believing in a supreme power. Of course he would always remind her that the way they idolised 'fate' could be seen as creating a new supreme being. He preferred to believe you created your own destiny, but he knew Tad loved the story, and wouldn't change it for the world.

'One fine day in Douentza, the Dogon people took long ropes made of Baobab bark, to the cliffs of Bandiagara where all the boys who wished to fulfil their rite of passage to manhood would need to ascend the cliffs using their own strength alone, without falling or stopping. Tadelesh loved to watch the ritual, sometimes sitting with the elders at the base of the cliffs on the scree, and sometimes with the women on the top, shouting encouragement.' Ymarise glanced sideways at her son, but he opened his eyes wide again at the pause in the story.

She continued: 'That morning Tadelesh had decided to watch the proceedings from the top of the cliffs, so he had set off early with his mother, aunts, neighbours and grandmothers along the winding path to the top of the escarpment.'

'Tadelesh ate some sorgum pulp he had wrapped up in a Baobab leaf the night before, and leant over the top of the cliff to see who was going first. Tadelesh's Aunt Satimbe grumbled at him to take care but Tadelesh didn't listen. Suddenly his foot slipped on some loose rocks and he felt himself start to fall. He flapped his arms to try to stop himself falling over the edge but knew it was hopeless. As he started to scream a giant golden hand shimmered into existence at the top of the cliff. Satimbe and Katanga gasped as the hand nudged Tadelesh back into safety. It was not fated that Tadelesh should die that day. The golden hand became translucent once more, until all that could be seen were some golden strands of dust dancing in the sunlight. Tadelesh knew he was indeed blessed with luck. The End.' Ymarise closed an imaginary book and wriggled off the bed. She stroked her fingertips through Tad's hair.

'Do you think I have a golden hand, mum?' he asked sleepily.

'I'm sure you do sweetheart,' Ymarise smiled.

Tad sighed and rolled over, preparing for sleep. 'It should have stopped me falling through the bridge,' he said thoughtfully.

'Trust in your GGP sweetheart…and get some sleep.' Ymarise bit her lip.

Bracq flicked the antique light switch and drew his wife out of the room, 'He'll be fine.' he whispered.

*   *   *

Fraser stepped on to the encoder platform on Lunar 17 and waited for the moment when all his molecules would exist in two places at once for a split second, before they all chose to be in Europa. He always wondered what would happen if a few vital molecules chose to remain behind…maybe they wouldn't all fancy travelling today? Not good thoughts for the Interplanetary Liaison Officer to be having on a Monday morning.

He mentally reviewed his interviews so far. Yer and Elbeth Catenay were an odd couple, the husband being a very tall man with an expressionless, almost Lurch-type face, which, as he was obviously not dim, was perhaps meant to intimidate his business adversaries into gushing; while the wife was short but slim with a serious face and polite mouth with lips kept close together. Fraser thought Yer would make a good lawman. His first impression of Elbeth was that she had married with her head not her heart. They interviewed smoothly, their responses were polished and confident, and they sounded like a tight team despite being interviewed separately and with 'plants off. They also managed to avoid using any of the same phrases that would make it sound rehearsed. He wondered if he was paranoid to think they might have done just that.

El Omonv arrived with his second wife who had not been present at the ball, and they passed his first wife Dune Omonv as she left. Fraser had noticed the two women glaring at each other, but any animosity there would not incite either to steal from a third party. El did not appear to notice. He greeted Dune with amiable bluffness, and obviously expected Cailly to do the same. He came across as a jolly, overindulged, upper class blockhead.

Of course if any of these guests were to become suspects, they would all need an accomplice or hired help, since Fraser himself had seen the thief while all of this lot were locked down in the ballroom.

Bizelle Eastman had not shown up for her interview, so he would have to track her down later. The man mentioned in the newspaper article, Giles Brandforth, had turned up with his friend Artur, who then stayed on at the request of his parents to give them 'moral support' during their interview. They had all seemed to be harmless idiots. He hoped the insinuation in the newspaper about approaching nuptials was not true, for the sake of Tuula's sanity. If she liked any of these pompous eggheads, then maybe he'd been mistaken about the initial chemistry he had felt when he met her. Fraser screwed his eyes up tight and then rubbed his forehead, trying to get his brain back on track. The next interview was the hostess herself.

Mariposa Eastman came essentially alone, but only after a lingering goodbye from an old friend who had led her by the arm right up to the door of the interview room. Once free of his grip and out of his vision she appeared to correct her expression from frail wounded victim to business woman, without a trace of sheepishness. Fraser tried to assess which parts of her face and body had escaped rejuvenation surgeries but was cut off as Mariposa asked sharply: 'Shall we begin?'

'Yes, certainly we shall,' Fraser replied smoothly, lifting his eyebrows to Varn which could have meant anything ranging from "Did you just hear that tone" to "Are you ready to start?".

'Two days ago Ms Eastman –'

'Oh you should call me Mariposa,' she interrupted, 'it will make everything go much swifter I assure you.'

Fraser ignored the length of time her interruption had just cost her obviously valued time, and continued, 'Two days ago you were hosting a party with nineteen guests including yourself, is this correct?'

'If you say so. I believe my butler gave you a list of guests?' Mariposa inspected her nails.

'Yes, please thank him for his co-operation.' Fraser answered drily. 'Could you please relate to us the events leading up to my arrival at Nollerton House?'

'Well, as I had entombed myself in the safe room I really had no idea when you arrived, but I will tell you what I think…There is no possibility of any of my close friends being involved in this dreadful scandal!' Mariposa shuddered gently.

'Why don't you start at the beginning?' Fraser tried prompting gently.

'I don't suppose you would be interested in all my trivial preparations for the ball. It really isn't relevant. The first thing you *should* be interested in, is me checking my safe at 6:01, when I quickly realised that my beautiful Sunshine Yellow was missing, and that the safe showed a timed entry at only 6:00. You can imagine how scared I was.' As she finished her sentence she fixed Fraser then Varn with a steely glare, willing them both to acknowledge her account, but diminishing the likelihood of them believing her capable of such an emotion.

'You certainly did well to control the situation despite your unrest,' Varn added with a smile.

'Well, of course, somebody had to do something!' She again lifted her intense glare to Fraser, as if he should have known earlier there would be a robbery and been present himself.

'Can you think of anyone that may have held a grudge against yourself or your late husband?' Fraser continued smoothly.

Mariposa drew herself up to a less than commanding height, but still managed to inject ice into her voice, 'If you don't mind me telling you, young man, I think that is the most ridiculous question I have *ever* heard. Of course there is no-one. I've told you already, none of my guests are responsible.'

'Thankyou Mariposa, I think that is all we need for now.'

As the widow tottered off to brave the world once again Fraser shut the door and turned to Varn, 'What do you think?'

'That it could 'ave been done by any one of them, but so far we lack a motive. Shall I tell you about the two who could not make it to the party?'

'Only if it's good.' Fraser sighed as Varn rolled his eyes and turned to leave, 'No, I didn't mean it – tell me anyway!'

'Oz – nobody knows 'ees surname, comes from some godforsaken back water – watertight alibi without need for interview – he was logged onto grid at 'is own house. Cailly – you met her today, she is the wife of the mayor El Omonv.' Varn looked for signs of recognition from Fraser.

'Yes - leggy blonde, too young for him - I remember.' Fraser grinned.

'She was accompanied all night by friends who are willing to testify. She was at 'Le Bleu', perhaps you saw her yourself, indeed?' Varn paused dramatically, 'Ah yes, I remember, maybe your interest was elsewhere, hmmm?'

'Hmmm,' Fraser confirmed, smiling, 'something like that. I'll see you later ok? I've got some more interviews to chase up.'

Fraser sat at his desk and wondered if he had enough evidence to warrant a meet with Tuula Saussay. It was either that or trying to track down Bizelle, the thin girl whose holo showed a skeletal face that seemed to confirm all the rumours about her habit, that had been flying around the interview room today. He didn't much relish an encounter with Bizelle if she turned out to be a mini replica of her mother, Mariposa.

Tuula was on the invitations list, and they had chased up all the other non or partial attenders, which gave him ample licence to talk with her. Unfortunately he stood in the position of her alibi, which did seem to negate the need for a chat. However, if he was to tick all the boxes, and perform this investigation by the book, then he really should do it anyway. It really was the least required of an interplanetary liaison officer.

He smiled as he waved goodbye to the lawman at the front desk of the New Manhattan station, and walked with a jaunty step to Herve Saussay's headquarters. He was informed that Tuula only worked for her father two days a week, and would have been disappointed had the PA not also chosen to disclose that she thought Tuula volunteered at the Dome water recycling plant on some of her days off. She had said it with a twinkle in her eye, as if she knew there was a romance afoot, and Fraser tried hard not to smile back.

He navigated using his grid access via his 'plant, enjoying turning down streets that were new, and letting his eyes wander to the tops of the buildings and the dome sky, without needing to concentrate on what he was doing or where he was going. He caught a pod across town and narrowly avoided getting his trouser legs wet by jumping across the gap while the water was still sloshing.

The water recycling plant was a modern building with a flat imposing frontage in white. The reception was cluttered and the receptionist almost personified her own desk. She had a variety of old style tablet pens tucked behind both ears, hair had escaped from her bun, and she was engaged in licking doughnut sugar from her fingers when he arrived. 'Hmm, hold on a sec, right! Ok, what can I help you with?' she asked, slamming on a belated corporate image smile as she finished.

'My name is Fraser Moldonny. I'm a lawman looking for Tuula Saussay.'

The woman's untidy eyebrows shot up underneath her messy hair. 'Oh dear, nothing bad I hope?'

'No need to worry, she's not in any trouble. We just need to speak to her. Is she working here today?' Fraser wondered if this simple request might be beyond this lady's organisational skills, but after a moment he had to chide himself on judging the book by its cover.

'Yes, until three. She'll be either by the green roofs or the bioretention ponds or in a rain garden. Or if you'd care to take a seat I could just inform her to meet you here…that might be easier.' The woman took two styluses from behind one ear so that she could tap her own 'plant to subvocalise a message. She was one of those people who had never learnt to do it without screwing her eyes up in concentration.

Fraser smiled his thanks and strolled over to the white seats, from where he could see out to some kind of constructed wetland. As he glanced back at the receptionist, she had an odd smile on her face, and he wondered just what they were talking about, or even if they were still talking.

He heard Tuula's click of heels on marble before he saw her, and when he turned around he felt such a kick of adrenaline in his stomach he only just managed to engage his brain to greet her. 'Miss Saussay, thanks for coming. I'm here on official business.' He could have shot himself for stating the obvious. Was he afraid for her to think he might have trawled the town just to see her for his own sake? Yes. Very afraid. He grinned, and fell back on well-rehearsed lines, 'Is there anywhere we could go to talk?'

'Sure. I may be just a volunteer, but I have my own office!' Tuula sauntered away to the lifts and Fraser followed the rhythmical sway of her hips. He wondered whether every volunteer got office space or whether it was just part of the gift of being born a Saussay. He would bet heavily on the chance these thoughts never entered her head. He was so out of his league it wasn't even funny. He smiled; seeing those classy legs in front of him seemed to override his own reservations.

When he was sure they were out of ear shot, he leant in closer to whisper: 'But is it as tidy as your front reception, that's what I want to know!'

Tuula laughed and blushed slightly. 'Isn't she incredible? I don't know how she gets any work done! Mine is just round here. It's not spotless though, I have to warn you.' The door opened on a sensor and she fell into one of the three chairs, indicating a choice of two for him.

'Good,' Fraser tried to look innocent, 'never trust a woman that's too tidy, that's what my mother always tells me.'

Tuula breathed slowly to stop herself blushing again. She wanted to ask about his mother, but thought the blood vessels in her cheeks might give her away. He was here on business after all, not to have a natter. She tried to fill the silence, 'I heard you spoke to my parents this morning… I was wondering if I would be on the hit list.'

'Yep, 'fraid so. Did you know they came separately for their interviews?' he asked, a little surprised himself.

'That would be about right. They are both very busy, but in different ways.' She smiled fondly.

Fraser had liked Herve Saussay and his wife, but didn't think they were very compatible. He supposed Tuula must know better as she showed no strain when she talked about them as a couple.

Fraser tapped behind his ear and added a filename, 'I'm recording this, ok?'

'Yes, understood.' Tuula had to shake the image of prison cells just from that tiny formality. She rested her elbows on the desk and her hands on her bottom lip.

'No need to worry.' Fraser smiled at the sudden transformation to shy robin again, her eyes fixed on his face as if she would fly were he to move, 'Just a few questions, then we'll be done.'

'On the night of the Nollerton charity ball, what time did you arrive?' he asked.

Tuula let out the breath she had been holding unconsciously, 'I think it was about ten o'clock, most people had arrived already.'

'Okay, and what time did you leave, and who did you inform you were leaving?' Fraser continued smoothly.

Tuula looked at the table. Fraser quickly added: 'This is just a formality. We already know you have a tight alibi for the time of the robbery.' His eyes smiled at her, with one eyebrow slightly lifted.

Tuula tried hard to construct a coherent sentence, 'I think Bizelle guessed I was going, but nobody really *knew* knew. I think it was probably twelve o'clock when I left, maybe a bit later.'

'Ok, and lastly do you know of anyone who might benefit in any way from stealing a valuable jewel, someone in financial difficulty for example, or who may have held a grudge against Mariposa for any reason?'

'Bizelle fits all those categories from time to time. But I think her mother would give her the money no questions asked. I don't think she would care enough to find out what it would be spent on.' Tuula frowned.

'You're referring to Bizelle Eastman's habit, I suppose?' Fraser interjected, for the sake of continuity on the recording.

'Yes. Although I don't know her that well. We've never been close. She isn't much of a one for small talk at parties, and that's all I was attempting to do that night.'

'Attempting?' Fraser asked.

'I don't think she likes me much. Well, no, I'm not sure she likes anyone much at the moment. Not that I want to implicate her in any way…I didn't mean that. I just think she has problems just like anyone else.' Tuula grimaced at Fraser, knowing she made a hopeless interviewee.

Fraser tapped his device again, 'you can relax now, formalities are over!'

'Oh, that was hideous. I hate being recorded!' Tuula exhaled in an exaggerated fashion.

Fraser laughed, 'You were fine – it's just loose ends anyway. But don't think you're off the hook yet – I have some questions of my own to ask you!'

Tuula ignored the fluttering in her stomach, 'Such as…?'

'Such as did you wangle me an invite to your parents' party to try and show me up with your posh friends and your alleged fiancé?' Fraser leaned forward over the desk.

'He is absolutely not my fiancé for a start! He is the most buffle-headed buffoon I have ever had the misfortune to be associated with!'

'Hmm, mental note, look up buffle-headed in dictionary.' Fraser began, smiling, then changed tack, 'So you heard those rumours then?'

'Seeing as they were plastered across the news I could hardly help but notice!' Tuula sighed exasperatedly, hoping he had forgotten his other question about getting him an invite.

'You do know I own a tux don't you? And now that I have seen what type of party you people throw I think I can manage not to embarrass myself.' He shook his head in mock reproof, 'Naughty, naughty trying to show up your local law enforcer!'

'I did not! Of course I know you own a tux! It wasn't like that!' Tuula struggled to absolve herself.

'Ah, so you did get me an invitation.' Fraser smiled smugly. 'Now how are you going to stop all the inevitable speculation in this poor country boy's heart?'

Fraser ducked as a paper slim digital photo frame narrowly missed his head. 'If your morals were as good as your reflexes you wouldn't be forcing confessions out of innocent females!' Tuula raged at him, caught in her own embarrassment. 'Now get out before…just, out you go! I've got work to do!'

'Before what?' Fraser asked standing by the sensor to open the door. 'Just what other dark secrets are you hiding in there?' He paused. 'But I'm afraid I'll have to wait to find out at the party! I've got work to do too!'

Tuula scowled at him 'Don't look so happy with yourself, DI Moldonny.'

Fraser picked up one of her hands and shook it, smiling. 'I wouldn't dream of it. Thank you for your time and your co-operation, Miss Saussay.'

Tuula waited until her heartbeat had returned to normal before she also left the room, her white coat flying behind her with the speed of her walk.

5 BLISS

Amiette Vandril had woken that morning feeling fresh and invigorated. She felt satisfaction at all the little things from the softness of her pillow to the way her back cracked when she stretched. If she had wings she would have flown down the stairs. The world seemed to have taken on a shining clarity overnight…this was obviously what a good night's sleep did for you. Today was her only son's last day at home before he left for university, and it was her only purpose to make his last day with her as good as it could possibly be. She felt like a perfectly tuned violin, tense with energy at what she was going to do this morning, and humming with the unity she felt for the universe. How lucky was she to have a son like Genilh! What a fabulous time of life she was in! What potential there was just ahead of her! A new life, new possibilities!

'Don't go on the 'xeno with your bare feet Genilh, I've just advanced it!' Her voice sing-songed from the kitchen where she was chopping root vegetables with a vigorous hacking motion powered from the elbow.

'I know mum, I'm not six years old. I can smell that stuff six blocks away!' Gen answered in the sophisticated monotone that only a teenager can produce.

So much to do! 'Hummm, hmmm, la da di da! Somewhere! Beyond the sea! La la – happy for meeee! Da da dee ah di da, somewhere!' Amiette paused, and subvocalised a command to turn the music down, 'Genilh!' she called.

'Yeah?'

'I'm going to sort out the attic before we go out, ok?'

'Won't that take ages?' Genilh answered, diminishing the strength of his voice as he came in from the garden.

'No, it'll just be a whip around. Why don't you pack your bags while you wait?'

'Nah, I packed them yesterday. I'll just play Tankoon.'

'Bet I'm done before you are!' Amiette sing-songed back without turning from her soup preparation.

At eleven o'clock Genilh popped his head up through the attic hatch. 'You done yet mum? We should probably get going.'

'Oh darling just look at what I've found – boxes and boxes of your Grandad's old holos of me and your Auntie Villa before she died! These should be sorted shouldn't they? I never get a chance to do this kind of thing! Look at this one with Villa in that stupid spotty dress! We used to fight over that all the time!'

'Yeah, nice.' Genilh went back to his screen. He subvocalised to his mate on the grid game:

'LOOKS LIKE I'LL BE ABLE TO PLAY YOU AFTER ALL.'

'I THOUGHT YOU HAD TO DO STUFF WITH YOUR MUM ON YOUR LAST DAY AT HOME, 'N ALL THAT?'

'NOPE. S'FALLEN THROUGH.'

'OH, OK. SEE YOU AT THE CHECK POINT ON LEVEL 2?'

'YEAH.'

Genilh knew from experience that a good day with his mother could be almost as infuriating as a bad day. He had come to terms with the fact that his mother was not a reliable woman. Occasionally fun, but not to be trusted. So he had spent his childhood taking the fun where it came, and never daring to hope that her fantastical plans would ever come about.

At twelve o'clock he sold the two tickets for the festival on e-bay and added the funds to his 'diveball lessons account' on the grid.

At three o'clock Amiette emerged with smudges of dust all over her face. 'Are you ready? Shall we go?'

'I think we missed it mum,' Genilh replied in an even voice.

'Oh! Well, it doesn't matter! This is your last day! We probably shouldn't waste it going to a festival. Let's sit in the garden and enjoy the weather.'

'Ok, I'll just go make a drink,' Genilh said, smiling a resigned smile.

'I know! Let's get out the old kaftan I found in the attic and make a tent...then we can drink our drinks inside like a sheikh!'

'Yes mum, let me just transport myself back to when I was four years old and I last found that fun.'

The sarcasm was not lost on Amiette. 'Come here you.' She smiled and pulled her son into a reluctant bear hug. He smiled despite himself.

He also smiled as they sat on the lawn drinking shrink wrapped green tea from the loft, and he smiled as he unpacked his teddy that his mum had left sticking out of his bag, and later he smiled as he tipped his imaginary cap at his mum before he disappeared on the padding platform.

Amiette sat down on the AC lid and flicked her fingers over the door sensor so that it opened just a fraction, with the ease of many years' practice. She used to keep an eye on Genilh even when she was sitting on the toilet! Tears slid down her face and made a detour around her wobbling smile at the cruel irony which dictated that when she could now finally pee in peace, she was wishing for a boy covered in syrup and flour to be rushing past the door.

3:26 am. The blue numbers hovered in Amiette's left visual field above her bedside table leaving no room for doubt. She looked at a faded board game sticking out from under the bed. It had been a present from her son, when he was at the age where he bought things for other people that he would quite like himself. Some people never grew out of that but Genilh had. Genilh was no longer living in this house in which she was trying to be asleep.

She wondered how many normal, sensible people were sleeping right now. She didn't feel normal or sensible. She felt so utterly bleak and empty that she would have categorised herself as a sub-species of humanity. She tried to remember her last day with Genilh, tried to recapture some of that happiness and animation. She couldn't even find the energy to try lifting her cheeks into the semblance of a smile. She couldn't remember how it had felt to feel good. Was that only three weeks ago? She tapped her 'plant on to connect to her son and then straight away tapped it off again. She didn't want to ruin his last image of her – happy and carefree, the kind of mother he could be proud of. He wouldn't want to hear about her problems...and how to describe them anyway? She didn't feel able to connect with anybody: talk to anybody even, she couldn't find the resolution to eat at every meal time, every mouthful felt like a superhuman effort. She felt ugly, unwanted, out of touch with life itself, as if she was standing on the outside, watching her body shuffle through the motions. She recognised this pattern. She had experienced bouts of post-natal depression on and off for three years before she was finally diagnosed with bipolar disorder, by which time Genilh's father had left for greener pastures. This was worse though, somehow. She didn't think she could feel any worse than this. The isolation seemed insurmountable. Her own hopelessness threatened to overwhelm her.

She tapped the 'plant again, and got as far as subvocalising Genilh's code before tapping it off. He had his own troubles to worry about. The last thing he needed was to listen to hers. Besides, she didn't want to lose him the same way she had lost his father. Ok, so she could feel worse than she did now, she could lose her only son; her only link to the world.

Her psychiatrist had told her she had to hold on to the belief that the depression would lift: that the bleakness would not last forever. How long had it been? Only three weeks. She knew the stats. Fifteen percent of all bipolar sufferers committed suicide after one month of depression. 'It will not last. It will not last,' she thought fiercely at the clock, now reading 3:42. Her friends had told her that she should reach out to them when she most needed to, to not be afraid of rejection, they would welcome her call at any time. What they didn't realise was that she had been sincere when she had accepted their help, back then, but the worse she felt, the more impossible it was to reach out.

She tapped her 'plant and quickly subvocalised her son's code before she could talk herself out of it. She listened to pure static for two seconds that felt like twenty, and cut the connection. The tears crowded down her face and pooled in her ears before wetting the pillow on both sides. What normal boy wouldn't be asleep at – she turned over – 3:58 in the morning? Everyone was normal except her. She didn't belong here. She hated feeling this way. She despised this disease in her life.

*   *   *

'Morning, you dried up raisin!' Edytha always tried to begin her session on a pleasant note, and nothing used to please her husband more than listening to her inventive insults. He pretended to ignore her most of the time, but she used to see his lips curl some days, and she knew she'd got to him. She was pleased to note her voice was wavering a fraction less than yesterday as she sat down on her rug in

front of the marble stone, and less pleased to see a hole in one corner of the garish tartan design, with some grass poking through to ruin the purple and blue straight lines.
'Don't know why I feel like crying every day when you obviously couldn't care less! Can't care when you are dead, can you? Wouldn't be surprised if you didn't care when you were alive either! Not that it matters now. Can't matter now even if I wanted it to.' Edytha stared heavily at the tombstone, trying to ring some kind of an answer from it. 'Steadfast! Ha! You are a coward! If you were brave enough you would not have died and left me like this – you would have faced up to our problems! All that training in how to be brave, and what good did it do me? Nothing, that's what! I'm sitting on a scratchy rug talking to a pile of dirt!'

Edytha watched a flock of birds undulating. They had no reason to be unhappy. No reason to be angry. She recognised the ball of emotion in her stomach now as partly anger. It was lots of things, but anger was certainly there. 'How dared you leave me!' she thought, 'How dared you reduce my life to sitting talking to the dirt! I hope that earth lies heavy upon your deserting body! I hope you hear my grieving every day!'

The breeze lifted a branch a few centimetres, and rustled the leaves, but the marble stone stood silent.

Edytha let out the breath she had been holding and plucked at the grass for a few minutes. She waited until her pulse seemed more normal, and then looked back at the grave.

Edytha gave in, 'Ha! Not talking to me again! Well, we'll see about that.' She smiled lopsidedly, as if suppressing a big secret with difficulty. 'I found FTT for you on computer today. What do you say about that?' She lowered her voice conspiratorially and leant in to the smooth stone, 'It had clever encoding on it too!' She waited for this to be absorbed and then continued, 'I probably would have cracked it too by now if I didn't have to come down here and tell you about it. And yes, I know you would have done it quicker than me, padlo! You always were whizz with the codes!' Edytha leant back, satisfied that wherever his atoms now resided, they were all of them burning with curiosity about that message. 'Me, I think FTT relayer is on the blink. Who's going to be sending you messages at your age in code? I'll find out though. Soon enough I always find out! Never forget that Oszkár, wherever you are.'

Edytha turned her face up towards the orange glow, and felt a strange thought begin to find a form in her mind...she was glad it was him, and not her. Between the two of them, she was immensely relieved that she was here, breathing the air, feeling the orange sun, and dealing with the barely suppressed rage and grief. She let out a long breath and let the thought crystallise. Did she have survivor's guilt? No! Would he have dealt with it better than her? No, probably worse, she decided. He would not only have spurned the kindly offered help of the neighbours, but would probably have told them where to shove it. She wondered whether he had been more ready to die than her. Was it better he had gone because he had become so embittered with life? Would he give her hell for even *thinking* that it served him right he was the first to go? Probably. He would probably tell her to stop her damn existentialist thinking and go do something useful!

'Well, I did do something useful actually! I bought cabbage and bacon from that dismal looking shop over there!'

Edytha threw a glance to the far side of the field of plots

where the smooth pod canal was liberally sprinkled with run down shops: a grocers, a dispatch depot, a pharmacy, a rest-eat with grid access. The town planners had thoughtfully placed some malleable seating along the pavement for anyone unfortunate enough to want to spend their resting moments admiring the scenery of dead men's graves and dying businesses. Pods hardly ever came here, Edytha knew from bitter experience. The waterway was untroubled by traffic. Try as she might Edytha had never managed to rid her mind of the hyper-observancy taught in her early career, and now, as she looked along the line of seats, a small lady caught her eye. Female, age: possible mid-forties, brown hair, bloodshot eyes – lacking sleep: reason unknown, distinguishing mole above left eyebrow, no make-up – maybe she was careless of her appearance. The silent monologue flashed through her mind in under a second. She had smiled to the woman as she entered the shop over an hour ago, and then smiled again as she left – a slightly deeper but no more meaningful smile, to indicate that she recognised her from the previous time. Edytha swept the ground for exits and quickly identified four strategies that would get her quickly away from this spot without being followed, one of which felt water tight. She felt safe. She still knew her job, even if she was getting on in years. That FTT must have got her spooked. The woman still hadn't moved. In fact, rather than trying to appear nonchalant as most surveillance teams would, she appeared to have her head in her hands…not the typical behaviour of a spy. More of a seriously unhinged woman trying to lose herself for a couple of hours. Edytha felt a little sympathy for that right now. Not much, however. Nobody got anything useful done by rocking themselves in a foetal position for hours on end.

'Oszkár!' Edytha spoke, focusing on the part of the engraving which bore his name, trying to instil some of his personality into the shadows of the carvings. 'I think I should probably go. Don't know why I feel I have to tell you that, you old goat! And don't think I don't know how you laughed yesterday when you saw me get all the way across field only to come back and say it out loud. I know you!'

Edytha mentally corrected herself, I knew you, would be a more accurate response, but she didn't feel ready to say that out loud yet. Just when you felt a little buoyed up, something else popped into your brain to bowl you over again. Such was life. 'You got it easy. It's me you should feel sorry for! Me left with all the emotions! Me left in this stinking hole of a place!' Edytha stopped and placed her fingers to her mouth as if to take back the words. Wasn't that exactly what she had suspected he was thinking most days? And hadn't she hated him for it? She took several breaths using her diaphragm, controlling her heart rate as she did so. She wasn't like him. She wouldn't become like him. She wouldn't resent being here and wish her life away. She was blessed to be the one that lived. It was just a pity she couldn't tell him so. And so she had talked herself into a conundrum again: if he was here to tell, she wouldn't need to tell him.

Edytha got up with some mild assistance of hands on knees. Good job Oszkár hadn't got the knee replacement after all. She firmed her lips against such thoughts. No good thinking of what was gone. Think ahead instead.

She walked briskly to the edge of the grass, and then slowed as she crossed the waterway on an old-fashioned black tarcrete bridge with no sides. She watched the woman who had given up her rocking pose, but was now staring closely at her own shoes, still seemingly oblivious to outside scrutiny.

Edytha took the direct approach, not being one to mince matters. She sat down next to the woman and kicked her in the ankle. This seemed to win her attention, but no other response. Edytha would have enjoyed a battle of words in her current mood, but instead the face turned towards her looked a little blank, a little confused, but mostly tired.

'You should watch what you're doing.' Edytha grumbled, giving it one last shot.

'Sorry. Miles away I guess.' The woman now shifted her attention to the sky, which was, in fact, the high arch of the dome, keeping out the freezing winds and partly subduing the orange light.

'I'm Edytha.' She voiced loudly, wondering why the woman wouldn't keep her attention somewhere between the ground and the top. 'I come here every day, to visit –' she stopped herself from using one of ten insults that sprang to mind – 'my husband.'

'Oh,' and then, 'Oh, I'm sorry,' as she realised what was over the other side of the canal. Funny how you could stare at something without really seeing it. Of course, she wasn't really sorry at all. The rather dumpy woman next to her felt a bit like a fly on the arm of her depression, that she would soon flick off to be alone with the crappiness of it.

'You don't sound sorry. You sound abstracted.' Edytha voiced her observation, not even sure the woman was taking anything in. 'Well, I guess "I'm sorry" is better than nothing, not as good as a name when I go to trouble of giving mine, but there you are.'

The woman sighed inwardly, the fly on her arm was making her itchy again. What did this woman know of pain? So she had a dead husband. Who cares? At least she wasn't dead inside. At least she didn't feel her way through the day like a shadow in the mist. She was a little surprised to find herself mildly annoyed with this woman. Which was new, she hadn't felt anything apart from apathy for most of…what? Four days? A week? That probably meant she wasn't supposed to die today. She got up to get on the approaching pod. Then remembering something, she turned back to the small plump foreign woman with the firm face, 'My name – it's Amiette.'

6 DISAPPOINTMENT

'Daaaad?' Tad started hopefully, 'can I go to the Slide Centre for my birthday?'

'Your birthday Tad? When's that then?' Bracq answered casually.

Tadelesh rolled his eyes at such lousy subterfuge. 'Dad, you said you were going to ask mum! You promised me you would talk about it with her!'

Bracq smiled with amusement at his son's excitement rather than happiness at what he had to say. 'Well as it happened, we did speak about it, but I'm afraid it's still 'no', Tad. The Centre is just too expensive.'

Tad's voice crept up half an octave, and doubled the pace, 'But we went there last year for my birthday, and now that they've got the new four person mud slide everyone wants to go! Frel says he's probably going for his birthday!'

'Well, that's fine then – you'll get to go with Frel,' Bracq reasoned.

'But, *please* Dad, it won't be the same! If it's your birthday you get three queue jumps and your face on the vid slide for free! *Pleease!*'

Bracq sighed. 'Sorry Tad. We'll have your party here like we planned. Anyway, your mum's already gone to a lot of trouble with food, and hiring that virtual game! You shouldn't be so quick to dismiss what you have, Tad.'

'Oohhh, but-!'

'No buts Tad, that's enough!' Bracq rarely had to lay down the law, but he could when pushed.

Tad stomped upstairs. He recognised just enough of the truth to make the remonstrance all the more hideous. He knew his mum had started getting things ready, but he wanted a *Centre* party! When he thought of it yesterday it had seemed like the perfect answer. Pink leg casts would be instantly forgotten in the face of such a cool birthday. And now it was all going to be ruined. Just because his mum had bought some paper plates and hired a lousy game.

Ymarise fixed her smile yet again and entered her son's room. It clearly wasn't enough that Tad was being revolting over his birthday, she had to ride the brunt of her husband's guilt over shouting at Tad. Bracq's bad mood seemed to have settled over the house like a plague. As she peeped cautiously round the door a small part of her brain was wondering why her son wasn't apologising to her, and why her husband wasn't trying to help alleviate her guilt instead of wallowing in his own. She dismissed the treacherous thoughts. A family did not survive on bitterness. 'Tad?' She asked, brightly.

'Uh?' Tad answered somewhat obliquely, without turning around. He blinked his eyes rapidly, but Ymarise had caught the wobble in his voice and was already laying aside her own emotional state for the far more worthy cause of cheering up her little boy. She idly wondered if her protectiveness would become less fierce as he grew up, and decided she wouldn't want it to diminish anyway. She sat in silence next to him, one hand went to stroke his hair, which he immediately shrugged away from. She waited. Tad sighed and rested his head against his hands, then almost immediately sat up and stated the obvious: 'It's so unfair.'

'Hmm.' It was a fairly non-effusive answer, giving very little cause for him to be annoyed by parental hyperbole (your nose will fall off if you keep that frown going too long) or embarrassed by excessive sympathy (my poor little shnuckums, come give mummy a kiss).

Ymarise sensed him coming out of the downward spiral so thought she'd probably get away with mimicking his face. She pulled her mouth into a giant sulk, then used her finger tips to pull it into a smile. Tad rolled his eyes, but she could tell he was holding back a smile. 'How about tomorrow morning we go buy some goodies for your party before school and I'll drop you off rather than catching the school pod?' She waited for the significance of this treat to sink in.

'So I'll get to go in the back gate?' Tad opened his eyes wide, 'And I won't have to wait to get signed in?' For the second time tonight his voice was on the up, but this time in anticipated glee. 'Which probably means we'll save six minutes of queueing, which means we can go in six minutes later!' He finished triumphantly.

He smiled hesitantly up at his mother, not entirely sure if it would be seemly to come out of his sulk so soon. 'And what kind of goodies can we buy?'

Ymarise put off the next maelstrom for another time: 'Why don't you go and draw the kind of things you want, and label them all neatly and we'll discuss it later?'

Tad let out an excited 'Yeah' and ran off listing his possible treats until his words were a faint jumble mixed up with crashes and bangs as he searched for a notepad and stylus in amongst his toys.

Later that night when Ymarise dimmed the lights in his room, she saw a screen jammed with colourful drawings resting under his chin and the stylus held loosely in his curled fingers where he had fallen asleep still pondering the many delights in store. Her insides went soft and warm with love as she eased the pad out and saw the creases it left in his pale face. She could just make out a miniature version of herself and Bracq enclosed in one box, and drawings of some of his friends that she recognised, and others that she didn't in a separate box, surrounded by as many presents, foodstuffs, toys and surprises as his imagination could muster. He had drawn himself twice, once next to his mum and once with all his friends. Both were labelled in his meticulous handwriting, and both were smiling.

The next day Tad ran to the school gate four minutes late. 'I *told* you it was ten minutes!'

'No, monkey, you told me six minutes!' Ymarise kept her stern face on despite the teasing words.

Tad smiled reluctantly, not only did he have extra time at

home, but he now got to go into school late! Bonus.

'Don't forget to apologise to your teacher!' Ymarise called out in parting. She could hear similar advice being given to several other stragglers who were running into school late: 'Tell her the pod into town was running late' and 'You'll be alright – it's only because your brother was sick.'

Ymarise checked her watch and mentally swapped one set of deadlines for another; she straightened her spine and headed for work.

Tad ran down the corridor to find the school in complete chaos. Nobody was in their classes yet; there was a loud babble of excited chatter and everyone seemed to be crowding around a poster and a large spinning orb. He couldn't see any of his friends from his own class yet. He tried to look at the poster but couldn't get close enough. 'What's going on?' he asked in vain to no one in particular, but the older boys ignored him, jostling for a place.

He made a few more attempts, alternately jumping up and pushing before sitting on a rare vacant seat in the corridor. Tad was so teed off that the only day he had managed to wangle going in late to school something exciting was going to happen, that he tried to ignore the excited shouts and squeals as the comms system chirruped and the head teacher cleared his throat. 'As I am sure you are all by now aware,' the disembodied voice began, 'we have a surprise guest today. Alee Gretchid has kindly taken some time out from his busy schedule to visit us, and has offered five free tickets to the semi-grav climbing championships at the Kurchatov Crater! It is now my absolute pleasure to tell you the names of the pupils who will win those tickets...' Tad's heart began to race: how would they decide? What were the chances of him winning one of those tickets? The headmaster's voice continued: 'I am opening the ticket barrel that you all will have placed your names inside this morning...' Tad's heart now plummeted from his throat to his shoes. This was the clambering excitement. This was the chance he had missed. There was no point even listening now, his chances had gone from miniscule to zero with that one small sentence. He scuffed the floor with his shoes, annoyed with fate once more. The head teacher was spinning out his announcement like a pro, whipping everyone up to a fever pitch with insignificant details before he revealed the names. But there was the date of the event. And it was very significant. It was the Saturday they had picked out for his birthday party. His Dad had booked his time off work. He had given the deposit. Tad had the invitations set to send on his plant – he was going to do it this morning.

Tad listened again in earnest. Not his friends, he prayed. 'Not Frel. Not Frel. Not Frel.' he thought feverishly.

'And our congratulations go to...Jack Frellish!' Tad's heart sank. What would be worse, having his party without his best friend, or cancelling his party altogether? 'Well done Jack!' The head continued, unknowing of the damage he had done, and continuing in a chipper tone, 'And the second ticket goes to... James Birch! Fantastic James! And last but not least, the final ticket goes to...'

Things could get no worse for Tad. His life was ruined. '...Aaron Plesser!' the head announced, to a chorus of whoops. 'Those boys I have just called, can you make your way to my office for your tickets. The rest of you, off to class now please!'

Things just got very worse.

Tad sat by the window in his first class – Maths. He swallowed the threatening tears and pretended to be bored and stare out the window so he didn't have to talk about it to Frel. He missed the teacher's explanation of adding and subtracting decimals, and guessed all the answers on the test before he realised the results were being sent home.

That evening Bracq dug deep and summoned yet more enthusiasm to his tone - it was only one friend for goodness sake! He'd like to see what would happen if he just sat down and cried about his problems. One of these days his boy would have to wake up and taste the real world. But for now…

'Anyway! It's your birthday tomorrow, so let's try not to get sad about it! He raised an eyebrow at Ymarise in silent enquiry as he subvocalised a message: *'PRESENT NOW OR TOMORROW?...THERE WON'T BE MUCH TIME TOMORROW…'*

She sent back *'SIGH… I HAVEN'T EVEN WRAPPED IT YET!'*

He won't mind, thought Bracq *'WAIT UNTIL HE SEES IT – HE WON'T CARE ABOUT THE WRAPPING!'*

'Dry those tears and come and see what your mum and I have got you.' Bracq took Tad's shoulders and directed them to the doorway.

'Wait here. No peeking!' Tad rolled his eyes and closed them. He must be getting too old for birthday surprises. At least now he appreciated not being able to afford the Stone jacket. He had told Frel today that he wasn't going to get one – so he might as well spend his money at the semi-gravs.

'Okay…open!' His dad placed a box in his hands, a wide flat box with a thin layer of tissue over it. Tad scrabbled through the layer of tissue revealing a large S on a natural rock background. Tad felt his stomach lurch. Surely it wasn't…

He opened the lid and took out a jacket. As his fingers brushed the surface it changed from sand coloured stone to a whole network of fingers.

His parents looked at him with big encouraging smiles waiting for him to speak. 'Oh wow…thank you… I can't believe I got it!' He looked down at the jacket and put his fingers on and off the surface, watching it change as he did. 'I honestly can't believe it!'

'You're welcome my best boy. Come and give your old Dad a hug!' Bracq held his arms open and Tad walked into him, leaving the box behind.

'Do you want to try it on?' Ymarise asked.

'No not yet. I like the way it looks in the box – I want to keep it for best.' Tad thought rapidly, wondering how he would hide it from Frel, knowing he was now excited at having money to spend at the semi-grav championships, he didn't want to remind him of their little friendship…didn't want to risk seeing his disappointment…or worse to feel embarrassed when he realised that Frel had left all that behind him already. He wasn't sure he could take it if Frel joined in the taunting. ('Oh look, Aaron, Tad still thinks I'm going to be *his* friend. What a loser!')

He pulled on his mum's sleeve before she followed his Dad out of the room. 'I don't know if I'll wear it to school mum, I might lose it.'

'Don't worry poppet. We'll think about it tomorrow okay?' All very well for mums to say not to worry – they never had anything to worry about!

Ymarise followed Bracq down the stairs. He ducked his head under the archway and leaned on one arm on the kitchen surface.

'He did love it Bracq – he's just upset about Frellish, that's all.' Ymarise rested her head on her husband's shoulder and gave him a squeeze from behind.

'Hmm, maybe.' Bracq turned towards his wife and hugged her back.

Herve switched off the wall-mounted (and nearly wall-sized) television, and sighed. He had been enjoying the Semi-Grav climbing, but he guessed he could watch it later. 'What is it Saphia?'

'Since when do you call me Saphia? Are you in a grump?' His wife demanded irritably.

'Never with you my sweet! What can I do for you?' Herve always tried to ride the easy line with his admittedly high-maintenance wife. It usually worked out fine in the end.

'Well, I'll tell you Herve, I'm fed up with my life! None of my friends have to watch their lump of a husband spend the whole weekend slouched in the chair like some sort of outcast! I want to go to parties like we used to! Live a little! Not become two tortoises just because we're getting older!'

Saphia began to pace the room, flinging her hands about to add punctuation to her exasperation.

'Most of your friends no longer have husbands, Saphie.' Herve pointed out reasonably. 'Why don't you go out with Dune, or Assinia?' Although these two ladies could spit acid they were so bitter about their various divorces, Herve did see the advantage of them keeping his wife out of his hair for a while.

'Why do you always fob me off at the weekend?' Saphia enquired, a little more hysterically. 'What,' she paused, 'is the point' (more flinging of arms) 'of being married to you at all if you never *do…anything*?' She strung the last two words out into far too many syllables, with her voice raised to fever pitch.

'Well, my dear,' Herve began, unruffled, 'what do you propose we do about my tortoise tendencies?' There was usually an easy answer to these rants…a new ring she had taken a fancy to, a grand party to attend next week, a spectacularly expensive dress that had caught her eye. He waited for the hammer to fall.

'Your –! Oh that is just beyond anything! Have you not listened to a word I've said Herve? I'll tell you what we'll do about them! I'm leaving you Herve! That's what we'll do! And there's not a thing you can do about it!'

Herve sat forward in his chair, his interest aroused. 'Leave me, my sweet? Why would you want to do that?'

'Yes, why mother?' Tuula jack-knifed herself into the conversation with narrowed eyes. She had heard the arguing from three rooms away and she didn't like her father to be upset. Whatever she thought of her mother's temperament, she made Herve happy, and that was all that mattered. 'You seem to have had this argument well planned out from start to finish! Did Dune put you up to this?'

'You always take your father's side, Tuula! No she did not "put me up to this"!' Saphia made a venomous impression of her daughter; sneering her mouth into an ugly line. 'I happen to have come to the end of my tether with your father, and you may as well both get used to the fact that I *am* leaving him.'

'Is this about the Enceladus Ball, Saphie? If you really want to go, you just have to say the word and I'll be there!' Herve interjected, always wary when his daughter picked up the cudgels in his defence.

'No!' Saphia almost screamed, 'this is not about any ball! I'm just fed up! Fed up of not being important in my own house! Fed up of not being respected!'

'But you *are* respected, sweetheart! Isn't she Tuula?' Herve was ready to enlist help from any quarter.

Tuula raised her eyebrows sceptically but remained silent.

'Don't bring her into this. This is not her fault Herve, it's yours! And don't think I won't get your money because I know about Jaimey!'

'Mother, you've known about my half brother any time these last fifteen years! What are you playing at?' Tuula exclaimed heatedly.

'Don't you "mother" me! He was born to your father while we were married and that constitutes a violation of our marriage agreement! I know!' She pointed viciously at her own chest, jabbing it several times to make her point.

'It was Dune wasn't it?' Tuula asked her mother quietly. She could guess her mother would have no idea as to what would violate a marriage agreement on her own.

'I'm packing!' Saphia announced dramatically as she turned to waltz out of the room. Tuula could hear her berating the staff that had obviously clustered around the door: 'Well, if you must demean your professionalism by listening at doors, you might as well be useful! I need help in my room! Now!'

Tuula stood silently looking at her father's downbent head. He was slumped in his La-Z-Boy Magneto-III chair, giving the impression of being suspended in thin air. 'I'm sorry, Daddy.'

'Oh!' Herve looked up quickly, jerked from his self-absorption, 'Don't worry about me sweetpea! I'll be fine.' He paused, thoughtfully. 'She's probably not serious anyhow.'

Tuula rather thought his body language and tone of voice were demonstrating the exact opposite to what he was saying.

There was no way in space she would end up like her mother, living off another man's wealth, getting more and more bitter because life wasn't coming out as planned. Today was the day for a new Tuula. An independent woman making her own future! She had to move out. It was about time she moved out properly. She already had an apartment of her own, but she didn't spend much time there. It was easier to come home and have her meals cooked by the numerous staff hired to do her parent's every bidding. She opened her mouth to tell her father she was going to pack, and then thought better of it. Two women leaving in one day might be a little too much to bear. She would take a bit of her stuff at a time and retreat quietly.

'I'd better leave you two to it, then.' She said quietly in to the silence.

'Yes,' Herve replied absently, 'see you later pumpkin.'

She would still come over to visit, she decided, but she would cook and clean for herself. Yes, and she would enjoy it too. No more idling away her days waiting for something to happen, no more spending her father's money…Tuula stopped abruptly. She would need a proper wage. She ran upstairs and began to pack one bag's worth of clothes, makeup and odds and ends. She would have to stop volunteering for the water plant and start full time like any other normal person. No, scrap that. If she worked full time for her father she would still be using his name and his position. She would ask for a full time job at the plant. Yes, and she would need a toaster. As she hauled the bag down the back stairs she idly wondered how many toasters were in the kitchen. No! She must buy her own toaster. That would be better. Independently-minded normal working girls did not steal their parents' toasters.

She walked out of the back door and exhaled. Which way to go first? To her flat with her stuff? To a toaster shop? To her work to talk to her boss? To her flat to phone her boss? Finally she decided to avoid the stream of staff carrying her mother's things to a long black pod, and instead turned right towards the other gate. She would walk to the station instead, and catch a pod across town to her flat. A normal, honest-to-goodness public pod. She smiled to herself and shifted the bag to her other shoulder, boosting the antigrav. dial to stop the strap digging in.

She felt so euphoric she hummed to herself when there was nobody close by on the road. Not because she was embarrassed at the thought she would be heard, but because people who sang to themselves in her opinion were either pretentious hippies or people that were trying too hard to appear happy and unconcerned, which very nearly wound them up back in the first category.

As she whistled and hummed towards her flat she tried to gauge the exact moment when she would be within range to subvocalise her code to the door. She smiled triumphantly at hearing the click of the internal mechanism accepting her entry, and dropped her bag on the black marble steps for a second to push open the matching door. A marble door was all very well, but it did take some pushing, even with a few single phase motors to lend some strength to her slim arms.

Tuula kicked her bag in and then halted. She had a strange sensation that something wasn't quite right. Nothing seemed out of place, but the whole flat seemed brighter somehow. Maybe it was the sunlight at this particular time of day. She walked through the lounge, then began opening doors to her other rooms and poking her head in, just making her presence felt again after a little while away. When she got to the kitchen she almost screamed but the breath just got stuck on a full inhalation and the noise never got past her vocal chords. Just as her legs were turning to jelly coping with her indecision between fight or flight, the figure hunched over her kitchen table turned around and she recognised her half brother.

'Jeez! You nearly frightened me half to death!' Tuula

began, then shook her head when she saw him frown. 'No – not really half to death – it's just a saying. How are you? What are you doing here?'

Jaimey didn't smile in his eyes or with his mouth, but continued jiggling his right knee and tapping his left index finger on the table. Tuula knew he was pleased to see her in his own way, or at least that he was relaxed enough in her company that he didn't feel the need to stand bolt upright and then look at anything in the room but the person he was talking to. 'Hello NT.' he intoned, referring to his childhood name for her which stood for neurotypical. 'I've been working on programming a new level for 'Time Lords 5'. It's completely brilliant. You can feel the cold better than in any other walk-through game. I've been doing some of the 3D graphics for the snowflakes in level five: 'The Hunt for Lyragoon' and trying to set the timings for the cold hitting your face and then the sensation of melting, which is hard because everybody's face shape is slightly different and they have to slide down your cheek, so I had to –'

'Woah! Slow down Aspie.' Tuula reigned him in before he spent the next hour giving him all the detail of his programming job at Player. 'What I really meant was, what are you doing *here*? In my flat.' Tuula pointed her fingers down to emphasise the question. She had spent enough time in Jaimey's company to know how to deal with his Asperger's. You had to be direct, not take offence and not confuse. You had to have a plan and stick to it. 'Aren't you working from the office anymore?' she prompted.

'No. Michael Hannigan wanted me to change my hours. Michael Hannigan wanted me to start at 9:30 instead of eight and finish at a different time each day. Not a set different time each day but any time the business might demand of me, giving a weekly total of thirty nine hours not thirty eight and a half. You know I don't like nines: they're like infinity; cold and dark. I tried to tell him that thirty eight and a half was a nice reddy orange number with a warm glow, and that I would prefer to stick with that. He said we are all changing to conform with new directives and that I am damned lucky to have my job at all with my "disability" (the intensity of the index finger tapping increased as he mentioned the hated word), and I asked who was damning me and how can luck be damned anyway, and then Michael Hannigan called Mandy from Human Resources and we all sat in her office for thirty seven minutes, which isn't quite as nice as thirty eight and a half but still a nice icy blue, so I didn't mind that, but I didn't get all my programming done that I was supposed to. So now I am working from home and uploading to their server on the grid. Mandy says I can do thirty eight and a half hours a week for them from home and do overtime of half an hour on every Saturday, which is thirty minutes so that's ok.'

Tuula paused in her making of a cup of Mango & Mult juice. 'That sounds good. Do you want an M & M?'

Jaimey paused a little longer than was necessary, to make sure it was his turn to speak, 'Yes, please.'

Tuula slid a full glass across the table to him and sipped her own, 'What happened to your apartment?'

'Nothing happened to it, it's still there.' The finger tapping increased a little.

'Are you staying in my apartment at the moment?' she asked gently. 'I don't mind if you are, I'm just interested as to why.'

'My flat has a girl near it who wants to talk at me. She is very loud. She reminds me of the office at work. I don't like it. Mandy said it would be best to find somewhere more peaceful than the office to do my programming, and I thought I would come and stay with you here.'

'I can talk to her if you want…explain things a little…so she isn't quite so,' Tuula gave up thinking of an alternative word, 'loud?'

'No, thank you. I like it here. I cleaned the living room ceiling. I cleaned the top three shelves of the fridge as well, for me to put my coke.' Jaimey had a gift for missing hints.

'That would be why it looked different when I walked in I suppose!' Tuula smiled. He might have a higher IQ than she did but he would always be her little brother, and she felt like she should protect him. 'You can stay as long as you like. But I'm going to be around a lot more now, so if I get too "loud" you'll just have to tell me okay? I'll leave you a timetable of my working hours when I've made a few calls, so that you know when to expect me, okay?'

'Okay.' The finger tapping eased up a little.

Tuula slid into the chair next to Jaimey's. 'So tell me,' she started, 'how is cognitive therapy going? And do you still go to that other one?' She bit her lip, wondering what kind of a sister she must be to forget such details, and then automatically corrected herself, half sister. 'The sensory integration thingy?'

Jaimey stopped jiggling his knee for a second, then said into the silence: 'Sensory Integration Therapy, which is 'sit' for short, which is supposed to be amusing, being as that's mostly what you do, is no longer funded for poor attendees of CBT. And as I am a poor attendee I am no longer going to SIT.'

Tuula smiled at the joke her brother didn't know he had made. If there was one thing he hated, it was word play.

'And why are you not going to CBT every week any more?'

'I suppose the truth is, that I'm not exactly sure I *want* to change the way I think about things.'

'Oh, well,' Tuula screwed up her mouth sideways, 'I guess that's a serious obstacle to the therapy then.'

'It is.' Jaimey didn't like to think of anyone having to guess at anything when he knew the answer.

'Have you spoken to Dad lately?' Tuula asked with apparent nonchalance.

'No. Not for three weeks,' he paused, 'and two days.' Then without stopping for breath, 'It was warm and wet inside the dome, but the PIC'S were humming in the membrane, so I think it was actually quite windy outside. Dad stopped by to take back his convertor that I had borrowed.'

Jaimey glanced at Tuula's face when she didn't answer, which he hated doing because faces were too confusing. He remembered his therapist's favourite conversational tip…"If it seems to be going awry, just ask the same question back to them." 'Have you spoken to Dad lately?' He asked slowly, taking a risky gambit.

Tuula worried her bottom lip some more, wondering how best to answer. In the end her brain tried out so many different versions that when it came to the last microsecond of indecision, the truth popped out. 'I am almost certain that Saphia is going to leave Dad.'

'Why don't you call her mum?' Jaimey asked, missing the point.

Tuula often wondered the same herself, 'I was speaking from your point of view I suppose.'

Jaimey paused, to be sure of his gap. Tuula waited, seeing whether his brain had been trying to process other things while she had been talking. 'I don't like Saphia. It will be better when she isn't there.'

'Hmmm.' Tuula wanted to agree, but felt a small shred of loyalty to her mother remaining. She knew the less than tactful phrasing from her brother did not mean an absence of emotion, but she worried a little about the ambivalence of her own feelings.

'She's going to try to break the pre-nup with the cheating clause I think.' Tuula said softly, wondering whether he would understand.

'Well, she has plenty of evidence,' Jaimey responded, smiling.

Tuula smiled too, glad he was okay with it. 'I don't think it will hold up. You come over to our house all the time, and several people, including me,' she lifted her eyes to the ceiling in an exaggerated flutter, and Jaimey frowned, confused, 'can testify that she knew about you almost from the very beginning.'

'Hmm.' Jaimey answered, beginning to think about the coordinates for the programming that his sister had interrupted.

'I was thinking...' Tuula started.

Jaimey got up, took a bottle of coke from his shelf in the fridge, folded a square of absorbent paper in half and wiped it all the way round five times. As he counted in his head, the coke was left with an aura of gold at five, pulsing slowly.

When Tuula saw that the ritual had finished she continued, 'the only problem would be if she can prove I am an unreliable witness. It's a great shame you don't go out in public more. If you weren't such a social recluse, we would have a million witnesses!'

She checked Jaimey's face to make sure he understood she was joking, but realised he had subsided back into his work, his face once more passive, his eyes flickering between elements of his own personal screen, and his mouth murmuring numbers and programming code.

Tuula remembered the day her Dad had bought him a 'plant. He could finally completely submerge himself into a comfortable world of rules and numbers, with no confusing expressions and small talk to put him on edge. No distractions...he had been so relaxed...it was the first time he had managed a proper conversation with her. She smiled at the serious face of her funny little brother.

Okay, so back to her list. First things first, she should ring her boss at the plant.

Tuula wandered out of her brother's earshot to her bedroom, picking up her bag and dumping it on the bed as she went. She felt a wave of amusement that she would have to unpack it herself. Not that she had let any of the staff at her Dad's house touch her personal stuff, but if she didn't unpack her clothes straightaway on return from a trip, she was never appalled to find it had been done when she next entered her room.

Her bedroom in the flat was compact and modern, with no extravagances but equally nothing shabby. It was a bit like staying in a hotel. She would have to make it a bit more homey. First things first, she thought again, and accessed Grig's code. 'Grig!' She announced to the empty room when he connected, 'Your holo is still not working.' Tuula personally suspected her boss of tampering with his own holo image to cover his complete lack of social graces.

'Yours is though, so that will do for me!' Grig answered as per usual. 'What can I do for you Tuula?'

'I wanted to ask whether any permanent full-time positions are currently available at the plant?' she asked slowly, and then just to ensure she was being completely clear, added: 'I mean *paid* positions.'

There was a slightly uncomfortable silence, so Tuula ploughed on 'I recently decided I should be putting my energy into my chosen career rather than trying to balance that with certain family expectations.' Still silence. 'And as you know water management is my particular field of expertise, so I was hoping the plant might want to take me on in some capacity to more fully utilise my skills.'

'Stop, stop Tuula. This is unnecessary.' Grig spoke quickly, then stopped again.

Tuula waited for the final blow. How embarrassing to be practically begging for a job and still blown out. They had only wanted her when it was free. She wasn't worth a wage. 'Tuula, listen.' Grig started again, 'The kind of job you had at your father's firm…It commands a certain wage that I don't think I can meet. Besides which, you know, all my executive positions are filled, with no expectation of moving on as far as I am aware.'

He was letting her down gently. Arguing the lack of vacancy angle. At least he was trying to leave her some dignity. It was a shame she knew for definite there was a vacancy now that Trenya had taken a family break. Grig was talking again, and Tuula brought her focus back to his words.

'…It's just a pity you weren't looking for a more ordinary post, because you know we would love to have you doing Trenya's job. I just can't afford the kind of wage you would expect!'

'So let me have this straight. You *do* think I could apply for a job?' Tuula asked, doing a poor job of hiding her incredulity.

'*Apply* for it? No, you could have it, not a question about it. But it's only 12000 credits. Your father wouldn't hear of it. I wouldn't even ask you to think about it.' Grig left the last sentence hang in the air, almost wishing her to think about it.

'My father won't know. What I mean to say is, this is really none of his business. If you really would like to employ me I really would like to be contracted!'

'Tuula, Calm down a minute.' Grig insisted. 'You know Trenya managed all the rain gardens, that means mulching, and root maintenance! And she dealt with all the bio balance in the ponds!' he added, horrified, as if this clinched it.

'Yes I know – I've helped her with both of those – the Penstemon and the Ironweed. It's fine!'

'I know you can *do* it…the question is do you *want* to?' Grig asked, sighing heavily.

'Of course I do. I love all of that! Anyway I can always ask Dad to pull a favour and get me some nice weather when the roots need culling!' Tuula could almost hear the mental wince coming from her potential boss.

'Seriously Tuula. Your father won't know any of these details will he? The work…the wage?'

Tuula sighed. As a young independent female, it really shouldn't matter what her father thought of her income. 'No, he really won't know anything at all.'

'Thank the stars for that. I'll see you Monday. You can sign the contract if you haven't changed your mind by then.'

'Thanks Grig. I'll see you first thing on Monday.' Tuula smiled as she heard the click of his connection going dead. No social niceties from her new boss. She smiled wider. For the first time in her life she would be earning something that was completely apart from her family.

Jaimey saw the stream of data change on his screen as Tuula broke the connection. Monitoring all of his sister's communications and movements was simple enough. And necessary, when he considered the intricacies of his latest project. He had been told he needed complicated things to keep his brain busy, so it would concentrate less on writing

FTTs of complaint to HR every day, and more on his own concerns. His first project had been mostly hacking (his choice, not his therapist's). He had a gift for this and strangely enough they had been right, it had kept him busy.

He easily broke the government main sites and a few banks, but it had begun to pall. While he was looking for a real challenge he had come up against a firewall in a residential property, known to all the hackers he had spoken to online as "Fort Knox". The reference had been explained to him as some kind of old gold bullion depository that had been impenetrable back in its day. Quite by luck, while he was making inroads into that system, he had made an important contact whose level of understanding offered him a rare moment of hero worship. Not many adults inspired Jaimey, in fact he considered most to be incredibly stupid. Although his therapist Patty (and probably Mandy from HR) would probably remind him that it was not acceptable to tell anyone this. Personally he would have thought it should always be acceptable to tell the truth. He remembered how he used to love saying "Patty Parkwin Patty Parkwin Patty Parkwin" over and over when he had first gone to therapy. She had been the first person to explain to him that this sort of alliteration was a good form of relaxation for him, not a sign that he was an imbecile, but that sometimes it made people think that. It was exhausting trying to figure out what people might be thinking all the time. Mostly it was easier not to talk to people at all, and then you didn't have to bother with their guesswork, or mangling out the right words to reassure them. One thing that was good about Patty was that she was too self-absorbed to be bothered by his insults (his dad had told him this once, and he had agreed: he rarely meant to be insulting anyhow). She was also able to give him an unemotional perspective from other people's point of view, (namely her own). Maybe egotism was a necessary requirement to becoming a therapist. He would probably make a great one…apart from the endless talking.

Jaimey was not much one to trust in fate and its machinations, but in this instance he had decided that as he and his fellow hacker Oz had been thrown together, it had made sense to seek his new idol's help for his current (and most audacious) project.

*   *   *

Fraser jolted forward off the 'padding platform and was surprised to find his feet on a soft surface. He looked down at a deep red velvet carpet and was grateful that there were no guests to witness his clumsy arrival. Who owned private pads for space's sake? He looked around him. The pad was housed in an old fashioned and very ornate octagonal stone pagoda. The carpet on which he found himself was obviously a temporary setup for the party, crossing the garden as it did. He could see various guests making their way ahead of him to the front door. Although the last thing he needed was to get caught gaping by whichever members of the upper crust of Enceladus would be 'padding in next, he risked pausing a moment more to take in the beauty of the surroundings. The impressive cream façade of the house paled in comparison besides the new Loire glittering below in the glow of the warm and clear early evening light. He wondered, not for the first time, just how rich you had to be to arrange the weather for the purposes of a party. Certainly money had been no object when building this house. Some of the standard grey roof tiles had been replaced with what looked like rhodium: intensely shiny and slightly surreal, giving it a children's story book feel.

Fraser started a leisurely stroll towards the front door, his jacket slung over one shoulder. He noticed the mock-troglodyte dwellings further down the garden encrusted with rubies and blue apatites. Probably an expensive wendy house. It wouldn't have surprised him if they'd shipped the entire mansion stone by stone from the original Loire before the 21st century flooding. He breathed in the warm grass smell one more time before smiling at the staff at the door, and then relinquishing his jacket a little further on. The cloakroom staff seemed surprised to be directly addressed, even for something so trivial as a 'good evening'. They giggled a little and expressed the hope that he would find the jewellery display inspiring.

He snagged two glasses of wine from a waiter, downing one and ditching it seamlessly to steady his nerves. The second glass he sipped more properly, and realised it was actually quite pleasant: sharp but fruity. The name of the wine was etched in to the bowl of each wine glass. Either they would ditch these once this grape was out of fashion, or they could afford the nanotechnology to have them re-marked. "Cremant de Loire" it read. Of course, it would have to match the surroundings. It was probably vintage. Possibly priceless. Probably not the best idea to have necked the first one.

He looked around him and found Saphia easily, decked in orange silk and holding court with several men. Tuula was less easy to spot but once he found her, he found it very hard to look away. Her skin was pale: just as he remembered it. Her dark hair was twisted into a casually disarrayed knot, with tendrils escaping at the back only emphasising her long neck. She was in deep bottle green, from chest to toe. The fabric of the dress was softer yet heavier than those around her, it fell in gentle folds rather than stiff panels. Her style tonight only added to the delicate image he had of her. It seemed she could eschew the norm and still radiate quiet elegance, but there was an almost ephemeral quality to her that drew and held his attention. It no longer surprised him that there were rumours of an engagement. He was surprised she hadn't been dragged off to the nearest vicar by one of these rich monkey boys. As he thought it he scanned the room; there were at least ten males her age and more than half of them were looking in her direction.

He rolled the wine around his mouth, letting the bubbles ping at the back of his throat. Well, he would take any advantage he was given. He would be doing more than just looking.

'Tuula. Just the person I needed.' He remarked as he took her elbow and guided her away from her little group.

The lady in question was having a hard time remembering how to walk. Her heart had begun an almost painful drumming against her ribs. She told herself it was just the shock of someone suddenly appearing behind her. 'Well, hello to you too.' Tuula remarked, a little more sharply than she had intended.

Fraser didn't immediately answer, just kept moving until he had her far enough away from all the watching eyes. 'Do you suppose they'll be upset I stole you away?' He asked angelically.

'No, it was only Cailly and her friends,' Tuula answered quickly, 'they will all be analysing your character from afar, I dare say.'

'I'm not sure it would stand up to close scrutiny.' He smiled, a sturdy veil to smother any self doubt. 'Anyway, that's not who I meant.'

Tuula frowned, confused. Who else had she been talking to?

Fraser was wearing his twinkly eyed look again. 'Never mind.' He rolled his eyes. 'Anyway, it wasn't just a ruse to get you on your own. I really do need you for something.'

'Oh?' Her confidence slipped a little, but she was equally willing to be helpful if nothing else.

'Yes. Apparently there are some family heirlooms on display that are going to inspire me. I never can get to grips with new places very easily. It's my country roots, you know. I couldn't find them.'

Tuula felt the blush coming. 'A lost lawman. Hmm. I'll show you their trinkets, and then you can just not blame me when you see in which direction you are supposed to be 'inspired'.'

Tuula motioned the way down a wide gallery, trying desperately to regain her ability to think and speak and walk simultaneously. She lifted her skirts to climb down two carpeted steps and came to a stop in front of a well-lit cabinet. The 'Lovers Locked' eternity ring held centre stage.

It was a highly intricate and suggestive sculpture, embedded in a ring peppered with diamonds. The lovers in question were glittering with what looked like tiny diamond shreds highlighting their features. Their entwined figures leaned against a massive ruby. It did not look as if it could actually be worn. Perhaps that was why it existed in a cabinet. Or maybe it was just too expensive to be let loose on an actual finger. The caption read 'Legend suggests that upon seeing this ring, the next you give your full attention to will be the last.'

He glanced at Tuula who was not-so-subtly looking anywhere but at him. Her colour, he thought, was just a little heightened. 'So is it true?' He smiled, waving his wine glass towards the cabinet.

'Nope.' Tuula answered quickly, and hurried to explain, 'I first looked at it with Maiya Hirota back when I was about six years old, and we vowed to be friends forever and never get married. She moved away when I was seven, we never saw each other again, and I heard she was married for money at eighteen. Although that might be just Saphia's malicious tongue…she might be perfectly content for all I know.'

'Do you always waffle when you're nervous?' Fraser grinned and took a step closer. 'Maybe you just didn't give her your full attention?'

Tuula felt her heart slamming against her ribs now; time seemed to move forward sluggishly, the back of her throat experienced that strange plummeting lift sensation, but she still had ample time to notice his lazy twinkle.

His face inched closer to hers. He was going to kiss her. Probably. Surely he was? The butterflies in her stomach were unsure whether to flit in absolute fear or purest excitement, and still time was on their side…one sharp intake of breath…one tingle down the spine as his hand rested ever so gently at the back of her head…a quick wetting of her lower lip as her eyelids fell down…and then an explosion of sensation as, slowly, their lips met. She felt warmth cascade through her body just under the skin, followed by tremors of tingling. Her mind reeled with the influx of exotic information and her senses became both heightened and pleasantly dulled. So much so that it was Fraser who noticed the voices drifting up the stairs and pulled away first.

·

7 PRETENCE

'Do you want to escape before they get here?' Tuula asked, smoothing her hair down as she glanced hastily around her.

'Great idea, in fact I passed a lovely bit of garden on the way in that you could show me instead of this old –'

'Tuula darling! I'm so glad I caught up with you!' Fraser could just make out a murmured curse from his side as Saphia and Dune hurried towards them in a tornado of colour and perfume.

'And you are Detective Moldonny,' Dune interrupted with an over-bright smile. 'So nice to see you again. And in such different surroundings too? Didn't I tell you who it was Saphie?' She continued without pause and without taking her narrow eyes off his face, 'Is it strange for you to be so far from your normal stomping ground?'

'My stomping ground, as it were, is probably rather larger

than you would expect. I took on the interplanetary liaison role not so long ago. But I feel sure Tuula would like her friends to call me Fraser.' He smiled, with equal measure of charm and shrewd assessment, and crossed his arms over his chest.

Dune paused a fraction, before her own elevated self-worth kicked back in and she continued, 'So I hear you owe your invitation to your very brave feat! Are you at liberty to tell us exactly how it happened?'

'What a talent you must have for information gathering, to know the ins and outs of every invitation,' Tuula interrupted, 'I wonder if Fraser should rather be employing you, and then he would be at liberty to tell you all the details!'

'What utter nonsense you come out with Tuula,' she tittered, 'when you must know that I am a woman of independent means.'

'Yes, I think Cailly did mention the divorce settlement to me once.' Tuula felt her spirits lift a little at seeing Dune Omonv barely able to conceal her abrupt anger, but thought it might be wise to extricate themselves before the explosion. She headed for the carpeted stairs. 'If you'll excuse us I think we'd better –'

'Don't go disappearing Tuula!' Her mother linked arms with Dune and fairly dragged her behind. 'I still need to catch up with you, and besides, your father wanted to talk to you about something. I don't know where he is...' Saphie almost kinked her neck to scan the room in an exaggerated manner for her husband. Dune asserted that she had last seen him at the bar, while Saphie protested that he had been hanging around the entrance. Tuula used the confusion to suggest rather loudly that she might take Fraser to find a drink, when suddenly all three women stopped talking and stared.

Dune recovered her wits first. 'You don't have to take this Saphie. We can leave now! He's got some nerve, that man of yours! Do you need something?' Saphie was vaguely waggling her fingers in front of her friend's bosom, until they finally latched upon Dune's wineglass. She downed it in one swig without losing eye contact with her husband who was striding towards them.

'Saphie, my dearest heart!' Herve boomed, making Fraser wince a little before schooling his features back to neutral.

'Herve! How can you bring that -, that -, how could you do this to me in front of all my friends! It's beneath you Herve! I never thought to be so humiliated! I was never so thoroughly mortified! What possessed you to bring him here?' Saphie almost hissed at Herve. Jaimey's foot was tapping rapidly. His body was rigid.

'Steady on darling! What has Jaimey done to upset you? He would never hurt a fly!'

Jaimey stared just to the left of Saphie's contorted face and mumbled 'Hello Saphie. I don't like flies in general. I try not to get too near them, so it is unlikely I would ever, I mean I don't think I would hurt a fly, no... Hmm.' His voice trailed off and his gaze skittered to the arched ceiling.

Saphie also seemed to be avoiding eye contact with Jaimey, her eyes searching widely as if seeking inspiration. By now they had attracted a little attention, and she could see some interested onlookers edging closer to the drama. 'Oh dear, I don't think I can...Tuula I feel faint!'

Jaimey searched for his exits. Herve frowned heavily. Fraser raised one eyebrow at the firm and steady tone of voice being employed by the invalid. Tuula was the only one to speak: 'Don't be ridiculous mother! Jaimey's presence has never yet created such theatrics, which leads me to believe you have another agenda. And I, for one, don't like it.'

Dune stepped into the breach as Saphie moaned. 'Tuula your unruly tongue does not serve you well tonight when it is obvious your mother is unwell. I might say, overcome! It is more than a good woman can stand! No! Dear Artur,' she turned to include the gathering audience in her farewell speech, 'we have no need of assistance! I will take Saphie away until she is quite recovered from this horrible shock.'

'Shock?' Herve shouted after her. 'Diseased, more like, from being surrounded by a coven of crazy harpies!'

Tuula turned to Fraser and caught a look of wide eyed and frozen disbelief, quickly suppressed as he smiled and took a slow sip of wine. 'Sorry about that,' Tuula grimaced. 'Dad, this is Fraser. Jaimey, this is Fraser. Fraser, my Dad and my step brother.' She indicated each of the men in turn.

Fraser shook hands with Herve who had finally given his full attention to his daughter and what she was saying. He noticed Tuula whisper to Jaimey that he didn't need to shake hands if he didn't want to, and then saw him scuttle off to the bar. His speech earlier had been confused, almost childlike, and she was obviously protecting him. Yet he walked without any serious deformity or weakness, albeit in a slightly gangly and self-conscious way. Not that he would be denied any medical tech for a disability if he was Herve Saussay's progeny. But still most likely some kind of mental disorder, he surmised. He would ask Tuula about it some other time.

'And why?' Tuula rounded on her father once she had seen Jaimey safely seated away from anyone who might be tempted to try talking to him.

'Why? What's wrong sweetheart?' Herve asked, a little wary of his daughter's questioning in front of a relative stranger.

'Why did you think it would be a good idea to drag Jaimey into all of this? And I presume you actually did drag him here, either that or blackmail him with something to get him here?'

'Thought it might do some good. Have it all out in the open as it were!'

'It has always been out in the open within our family, and Jaimey has no need to be further pushed into this 'open'.' Tuula flung her arms out to include the entire party in all its garish splendour. 'And if you supposed this was the right way to work Saphie, then you are appropriately punished!'

'Let me get you a refill.' Fraser interjected, and slunk off before awaiting an answer.

Tuula sighed. 'Thanks a lot! There goes the only interesting man in this room – scared off by the Saussay theatrics.' Herve didn't get further than a stammered 'but' before the onslaught continued. 'Did you honestly think cornering Saphie with her own lies would work? In public? Public is where she fights best! Or maybe you wanted this tactic to fail? Were you subconsciously sabotaging your own marriage?'

Herve shifted his weight back to the other foot uncomfortably, thinking not for the first time how similar his wife and daughter could be, though neither would admit it. 'I would never willingly let your mother go, Tuula, you must know that. Whatever else is going on, my family is the best thing that ever happened to me...my *entire* family. Now, if you'll excuse me, darling, I think I'm going to be needing a drink.'

Tuula shot him a look. 'And who's taking Jaimey home?'

Herve swung around to locate his son, at that moment tapping his feet with such ferocity, he looked in danger of falling off the bench. 'He's happy enough, Tuula, leave him be! I'll take him home later if he needs a lift. Or he can sleep in one of the free rooms upstairs.'

Tuula rolled her eyes and walked over to Jaimey, arriving there just as Fraser placed a glass of coke in front of him. 'Didn't know what you preferred, so figured I'd start with the basics. I can take it back and add a shot to it if you prefer?' He glanced at Tuula, sensing she was in some way his keeper.

Jaimey looked at Tuula who inclined her head twice slightly. 'Thank you, coke is good.' he muttered, looking with determination at Fraser's feet. He wiped the condensation from the glass, and re-wiped, and then tapped his right index finger, without taking a drink.

'You want to go early Aspie?' Tuula asked praying the answer would be no, but feeling sure it couldn't be.

'I would definitely like to go. I don't really like it here. I have some better things to do at home. I mean, at your house Tuula. Do you want to share a ride back?'

Knowing Jaimey would not understand the subtleties of saying yes but meaning no, Tuula resigned herself to her fate. 'I would like that.'

She smiled at Fraser sadly. 'Sorry. I have parents attempting to divorce, a mother who wouldn't know decency if it smacked her round the face, I have moved out of my family home, and my brother has moved in with me...My life is nothing but a complete and utter mess!'

Fraser winked, grinning broadly, 'How many times do I have to tell you? Never, ever, trust a woman who is too tidy! Do you want me to escort you guys back?'

They both heard the tapping increase in speed behind them. 'I'd love to say yes,' Tuula whispered, 'but I'd better not. I'll see you around.'

'Okay.' Fraser whispered back, and placed a gentle kiss on her cheek that effectively stopped her lungs yet doubled her heart rate for a vital few seconds. 'I'll see you around.'

Fraser watched them go, Tuula's calm voice talking in a slow and logical way to her brother as they left together. He felt the heat of the chase quicken his pulse. He knew she was out of his league but he just couldn't seem to help himself. He swept his eyes around the room. He knew he could win her over all these chumbuckets. If only he could catch a break. He wondered about the strange little brother a few more moments as he finished his drink, and then slung his jacket over his shoulder and headed for the pad.

Fraser awoke to several alerts, flashes and vibrations. It took his brain a good few moments to distinguish each one and identify it, as he left the bliss of a heavy sleep reluctantly. He felt too old in those moments where his brain scrambled to make sense of his surroundings. Useless lawman he made at – what time was it? – 7:15 in the morning.

He touched his 'plant and took the call, pre-programmed for voice only prior to 8am: 'Yep?'

The LPDPF Chief Ops answered succinctly. 'Your case just got bigger. Another big heist. Same group of people. Some kind of ball on Enceladus I understand.'

'Ah.'

'Problem?'

'I believe I may have been present, sir.'

'Hmmm. That won't look so good if the media get hold of it. Do us a favour and wrap this one up smartly Moldonny. They'll need you over there first thing.'

'Yes sir, Mr Frethun. I'll be all over it.' Fraser screwed his eyes tightly shut and then opened them one at a time, trying not to picture the headlines. He'd have to speak to Tuula again though; he tried hard not to feel too pleased with himself about that.

As he shot around the apartment flinging clothes on he listened to an FTT from work including the Visual Transmission from Herve Saussay an hour earlier. He had locked up at around 7, when the last guests had left and noticed the missing piece then. He looked and sounded a little weary, but who wouldn't after a family crisis and a hard night's partying? He watched Varn's disgruntled VT with half an eye as he brushed his teeth. It showed his unshaven face, gallic grimace and gentle diatribe on the difficulties of being partner to such an intergalactic superstar of a lawman. Fraser smiled into his reflection and spat. He watched the water, air and toothpaste suck away, and headed for the pod to work. He would telepad from there and thus skip the commuter traffic at the central lunar pad.

He arrived as Varn was preparing to leave, and caught his eye.

'Wait! Eh eh eh!' Varn shouted expressively at the technician. 'One more, ehn?'

'Morning partner,' Fraser slid in next to Varn and suppressed a shudder at the bleeps warning of the impending shift.

'Attends...' Varn held up a finger until they appeared at the Saussay's private pad on Encaladus, this time minus the red carpet and with a distinctly chillier feel to the air. 'Et bien. You have been 'ere before, n'est-ce pas?'

'Should I even ask how you know that? Or whether I have any hope of staying out of the news today?'

'Little 'ope, I would imagine. Never mind. How is your little princess?'

'She left the castle! There's a family feud going on by the look of it. I'll introduce you to the father if he's still here. The mother is AWOL, but you're not missing much there.'

'You think maybe in-door job, ehn?'

'*Inside* job, not indoor, Varn. I'm not sure.'

'Losing your perspective, my friend?' Varn punched his arm lightly.

'Get out of it, old-timer. Let's get in and have a look-see.'

The door was opened by Herve himself: this time with a crisper tone of voice, but still sporting tell-tale bags beneath the eyes. 'Morning gents.' He shook hands as he spoke, 'Nice to see you again Fraser! It is Fraser, isn't it? I haven't mentioned this to Tuula or Jaimey yet, so I'd appreciate you waiting on that front just a little while. I would have told Saphie but she's incommunicado at the moment. You are welcome to inform her if you can track her down. Hah! She'll be with Dune no doubt.'

'Can you tell us exactly what was taken, Mr Saussay?' Varn brought them back to business.

'I can show you! Bloody useless plate left there in its place, same as happened to Mariposa.' He marched off, indicating they should follow. 'I can tell you, it gave me a ruddy shock, when all I wanted was to crawl into bed!'

'Here it is. Or was. The picture is in this leaflet.'

Fraser took his but didn't need to look at it. The Lovers Locked ring was conspicuously missing from the encrypted cabinet. 'I saw the original.' No other jewellery had been taken. It seemed as though someone was making a point. The old style dinner plate was lying in full view, with the same words sprawled across it: The Dinner Set Gang. Fraser carefully laid the plate in an evidence box using gloves. Not that he hoped to ID anyone from it. The last one had been clean as a click.

A half hour later, and much traipsing around long and

carpeted corridors, Fraser was convinced Saphia had taken it as revenge, and done a copycat job to cover her tracks. It was disappointing in a way, as his continued presence on this case required the real 'dinner set gang' to strike again. And he did want to stay with the case...For the satisfaction of finishing a job, he thought over and over to himself. Not because of a girl with a fragile little waist and long pale neck. 'Just a job,' he muttered under his breath as he stepped off the pod near Dune Omonv's residence.

A butler opened the door, but was sharply elbowed out of the way by Dune herself, 'Never mind that now Michael, off you go, I've got it. Detective! I thought we might be seeing you today.'

'Really?'

'Well, yes, although I would have thought you would have stayed well out of it. She's not going back to him and that's final! He's been an absolute...Well, I won't tell you just what he's been, because it isn't very polite –'

'Mrs Omonv,' Fraser interrupted when she drew breath. 'I'm afraid I'm here on official business. Is Saphia Saussay here?'

'Oh dear, official business, you say? Yes, of course she's here. Nothing too awful I hope?' Dune lingered with a wistful hope of further information.

'If I could just speak with Mrs Saussay?' Fraser indicated the door with his eyes meaningfully.

'Yes, of course. Would you like to come through? I'll take you straight to her.' They passed through several large doors, Dune gesturing theatrically at the final one.

'Saphie, dearest. It's the detective here to see you!' Dune exclaimed brightly, despite these facts being apparent. 'I shall get you some of my special drink from India, Saphie...very good for your health...helps with any shocks or upsets.' Dune smiled sweetly as she floated out of the room, no doubt to summon someone else to do her bidding.

Saphie sat up straighter and narrowed her stare at Fraser. 'What is this all about? Am I likely to suffer from a shock? Because I warn you I've had my doctor out to me all night with my stress induced migraines, and I really should have medical attention if you are here to deliver any kind of news but the most pleasant.' Her fingers gripped the scrolled arms of the antique armchair. 'Did you come from Herve? Is he reeling in shock?'

'I did come here from your house, but –'

'I knew it! Is he begging to have me back? Why did he send you? Did Tuula refuse to come? I swear to you, I fear I have nurtured a viper in my bosom!'

'Nursed?' Fraser ventured in some confusion, but at seeing the blank gaze he continued quickly, 'Never mind. I am afraid I have some news that you may find disturbing, but hopefully not, er, overwhelming. If you would prefer to have a friend present?' Fraser left the question hanging, hoping to avoid having to deal with a hysterical migraine sufferer alone. Dune entered on cue bearing a tray, confirming his suspicions that she was hovering on the other side of the door.

'Dune, just the person I need. The detective is just telling me his news.'

Fraser stifled the need to tell them that official police enquiry was not normally termed '*news*'. 'I came here to inform you that a theft has occurred at your house. Nobody was hurt,' he added quickly seeing two pairs of eyes widen, 'but the "Lovers Locked" ring is currently missing, and the same calling card has been left in its place. This second theft within the same group of people does make it more likely that someone with inside information is involved.'

'Are you accusing us of theft, detective?' Dune's tone of voice sounded almost strangled with incredulity.

'Can you tell me where you were at 6:50 this morning, when your own encrypted cabinet was opened?' He immediately countered.

'Well, as a matter of fact we can.' Fraser recognised that smug smile for a decent alibi. His interest picked up. If it wasn't these two messing about, the real guy (BMW, he remembered with a smile) was still at large.

'...and the doctor said he would rather not wait by my bedside all night,' Saphie was still detailing the ins and outs of her cast iron alibi, 'but he would add a medical monitoring device to the room...and because Dune was also feeling a bit out of sorts after the stress of last night he said he would be happy to wire her up too, which I thought was very decent of him. So, if you just ring my personal *private* doctor, he should be able to confirm my whereabouts from about midnight to 10 o'clock this morning, when I took the wretched thing off!'

Fraser thanked the women for their help, added his sympathies for the loss of so priceless a piece, and let himself out, thinking as he smiled at the butler how much more he seemed to have in common with their staff.

A brief conversation with Dr Phelps brought him up to date with the latest monitoring systems available to the rich and famous. Complete with DNA tagging. No get-out there. And yes, the doctor would be happy to transmit the information to his partner Varn Delot.

Back at the LPDPF centre Fraser rewound his conversation with Herve Saussay – one unconscious guard with a round mark on his face, likely will fit the upcoming analysis of a pestle from the kitchen found discarded on the drive. This BMW planned the heists carefully, but didn't seem to think on the spot very well. The angle and force used was of a panic attack, not a professional incapacitation. And who hit people with a historical pestle hanging on a kitchen wall anyway? The cabinet was accessed at 6:50 am – a similar time of day to the first heist. Unlike the first robbery, the cabinet had not been forced. The pin number was over 15 digits long and was known only to the Saussay couple.

Varn had tracked the only guest they hadn't spoken to from the first robbery, only to discover his recent demise. Funny how death could not only be a remote, non-emotional fact in this job, but also a source of annoyance. The end to a promising lead. Fraser sighed. With so many incontrovertible alibis and a high likelihood of insider information, he had to acknowledge it was unlikely to be a single BMW working on his own. Did the 'dinner set gang' relate to the people they stole from or the group that were breaking the law? He stared at the plate wrapped in shrink, willing it to give him inspiration.

He looked over the information he had received on the bounders: First class equipment. Known to be issued to new recruits at MI27. No known links between the company that supplies them to MI27, or the government officials themselves to anyone on his suspect list. This, at least was comforting. Every time Tuula's name was free from association he breathed an internal sigh of relief, and then berated himself for needing it.

How was this group getting their hands on government equipment? He checked the search he had started on the grid into descendants of the original dinner set gang. It was still awaiting additional information to track name changes. He subvocalised a command to cross reference all names found with guest lists and known associates, and then idly tapped his plant, bringing up Tuula's code.

'Hi' Fraser started, and immediately wished he had planned some things to say first.

'Hi,' Tuula's image flickered into life in front of him – she was behind her desk at work, wearing a deep blue top and the same white jacket he had seen before. 'I thought I might hear from you this morning. My father told me.' Fraser watched her face for any sign of animosity towards her parent but found none, maybe just a little tiredness instead. But who wouldn't be tired the night after a party?

'Good. I'm saved a job. We are recording this by the way.' Fraser watched as she chewed the corner of a fingernail and then abruptly folded her hands in front of her. 'Do you have a cast iron alibi like your mother?'

'Sorry. I only have my step-brother's word that I was in bed all night.'

'Is he available to speak to? Can you give me his code?' Fraser asked.

'We don't give out his code to strangers without warning him first. His therapist told us not to. And he was stressed last night as you saw. Sorry, he doesn't do well in social situations.' Tuula bit her lip.

'Okay, can you send me the therapist's code?'

'Sure, hang on' Tuula looked in to the distance, clearly subvocalizing a string of commands. 'Okay, it's done.'

'Okay, thanks. Business over – the recording's stopped – you can relax'

She smiled and rolled her shoulders, 'So...Did you get back okay last night?' She asked, then almost kicked herself for asking a lawman whether he got home safely.

'Yes, thanks,' Fraser grinned. Was she blushing? Hard to tell from the washed-out holo image. 'I have an offer for you...How do you fancy slumming it for a change?'

'I'm listening.' Tuula, replied, frowning quizzically, hesitant, just like the robin he had first likened her to.

'I'm offering a home cooked meal, and your pick of a movie. My place. 7pm.'

'Are you allowed to ask me out in the middle of an investigation?' She twinkled.

'Who says I'm not investigating?'

Tuula visibly took a breath 'Oh, sorry, of course, I ...'

'I'm kidding! You're off the hook. The truth is, I'm not really allowed, per se...Which is precisely why you should come to my place. I can't keep meeting you at all these public venues where robberies occur and not get in to trouble.' Fraser looked at the indecision on her face, and realised he probably shouldn't kid around so much. 'So you'd be doing me a favour really.'

'I'd be doing you a favour, by eating a meal that you personally prepare for me?' Her tone was sceptical; Fraser needed to begin a serious charm offensive.

'Yep – that's about the sum of it. A huge favour, in fact. I cannot go another day without seeing you and my venues are limited to my space, yours, or the dark places under the waterway bridges.'

Tuula smiled.

'Okay, here's the thing. I either have to order food to go and meet you in the rain under a bridge, or you say yes and come eat with me. You decide.'

'That's not a choice! That is going out with you or going out with you!' Tuula exclaimed, laughing.

'As I said, your choice entirely.' He smiled sweetly. If she'd never heard that trick before, no wonder those lamebrains hadn't managed to win her over yet. Never give a girl a choice you can't live with.

Tuula bit her lip, trying not to smile.

'Okay, too hard...Here's an easier one. Roast chicken or Tang Pai Lai take out?'

Tuula laughed, 'Okay I give in, the roast chicken won me over!'

Fraser pretended to smack himself in the head 'Jeez, why do I never listen to my mother?..."Always lead with your strongest suit son," she tells me...if I'd realised roast chicken was my gold card I'd have played it first and saved us both all this anguish!'

Fraser leaned back in his chair, serious again. 'So, seven then. Do you want me to come get you?'

Tuula almost drowned in the sudden intensity of his eyes. 'Er, no. No, I'll get there. That's fine – just give me your address.'

'That's okay – I sent you an FTT half an hour ago with my address.'

Fraser just had time to see her shocked expression before he clicked off the holo. He smiled to himself, as satisfied as any schoolboy the first time they realise someone fancies them rotten.

Fraser was not one to revel long in his success. He initiated a call to Jaimey's therapist, and hung up twenty two minutes later considerably less tolerant of the variety of human conceit to be found in the universe, than he had been before. Ms Parkwin: founder and owner of 'World Of Therapy'©, was in every way beset by difficulty and was to be praised for her commendable efforts, her innovative methods and her personal diligence and dedication. Ms Parkwin painted a vivid image of the kind of delicate balance of therapy that has enabled her client to live any semblance of a normal life. Fraser took her monologue with a pinch of salt to counter her drama queen come entrepreneur style, but never the less, he left the conversation with a huge respect for Tuula and a greater sympathy for Jaimey, whether it was for his condition, or his inability to escape this woman's conversation, he wasn't quite sure.

Ms Parkwin tapped her long fingernails on her large and clean desk for a moment as she summed up the conversation in her head. She had given a good account of herself. She had sounded professional and knowledgeable. She had given the man access to all the client's records and attendance schedules. Yes, she should probably have mentioned that he failed to attend his last two sessions, the last one scheduled for that very morning, blast the boy, but was it clinically relevant? No. Nobody failed to attend sessions at 'World Of Therapy'©. It gave out the wrong image entirely. Far better to stick to the medically relevant facts. Yes, it was a job well done. She opened her holo screen and read the mantra that was saved to her desktop: 'I want to succeed. I have everything I need to succeed. I am everything I need to be to succeed. I will succeed!'

Fraser had a similar, but less scary, monologue with himself. He idly considered the damage to his potential relationship by being on this case, and the damage to his case by starting this potential relationship. He felt guilty about all the inside info he would be getting from Tuula that evening on the pretext of chatting. But then he remembered his excuse for seeing her was almost always bound up in the case so he wasn't about to lose that edge.

The door chime rang just as he was decanting wine. Fraser wasn't madly keen on wine but he did know enough to realise a good red needed air. Trouble was he had no fancy decanter…so he had spent the last five minutes pouring it between a large pan and a vase. It surprised him then that the sound of the door could startle him enough to create a slosh over the edge of the wide pan. He licked wine from his hand as he walked to the door.

'Hey!'

'Hi' Tuula indicated a bottle of white wine in her hand – an expensive one that came with an instant chill wrapper, 'I brought wine – white as we were having chicken.'

Jeez, what a schmuck, Fraser thought, of course it was white with chicken…Never mind, he would shove it in the gravy. He felt sure the gravy would benefit enormously from aerated red wine. 'A women who brings me gifts! This is what we like. Come in. Fraser deliberately waved her past him as he held the door so that she had to turn sideways and shimmy past him in the narrow entry hall. A guy had to take his pleasure where he could.

He followed her into the living room and took the bottle out of her hands. 'Stay! I'll be back in a minute.'

He hastily hid his decanting implements and added a splosh of wine to the gravy bubbling away. When he returned with two full glasses Tuula was looking at a large family picture from a few years back. She put it down to accept the glass from him and took a large gulp.

'Drinking for courage Miss Saussay?' He enquired with a smile.

'Drinking for survival more like.' Tuula placed the glass down but immediately searched for something else to occupy her hands, she wandered round the room, idly touching the leaves of a plant, the edge of a table, the edge of a –

'I wouldn't touch those, they're in their cases but they are real.'

Tuula jumped slightly and snatched her hand back. 'Real samurai swords? Cool. Where did you get them?'

'One of my friends on the force knew I had a thing for vintage items. That is the oldest artefact I have.'

'Wow.' Tuula smiled at him, a little nervously, she picked up her glass and fiddled with the stem. He was unsure if the weapon or the sudden lack of conversation unsettled her.

'Shall we eat? It's all ready. Are you hungry?'

'Famished!' Tuula rubbed her stomach and Fraser wondered how she could last from one minute to the next with so little 'reserves'. 'It smells great by the way.' Tuula had to shout towards the kitchen as Fraser was busy bringing things through.

'Where did you learn to cook?'

Fraser smiled fondly as he thought of his mother. 'My mother was happiest in the kitchen. It might have been her Italian roots. She told me she would have taught her daughter to cook but she only had boys and she couldn't bear to think of us wasting away before we got married.'

'You have brothers? Tuula paused to sip her wine, 'This is really good by the way.'

'What, your wine or my chicken?' Fraser laughed.

'Your chicken,' Tuula rolled her eyes and smiled, 'but the wine is pretty awesome. So - how many brothers?'

'Two. One in the army and one in IT research. Both on

terra, but in secure facilities. Neither of them very good looking so you can rest easy.' Fraser smiled a lazy smile, 'You got the pick of the bunch.'

'They weren't with you when we first met?'

'Nah, they couldn't get leave. And they thought it was extremely amusing knowing I was going to be stuck with my idiotic cousin all night with no relief, thanks for reminding me!'

'Are they in that photo over there?'

'Yup.' Fraser pointed them out to her. 'I'm not sure I like all this attention on my siblings.'

Tuula tried to hide a smile. 'What was his name again? The tall one? Was he the army one?'

'Seriously? We're going there are we?' Fraser narrowed his eyes, but smiled at the same time.

Tuula grinned, 'Mathew was it? He looks nice.'

'Mathew is in the army – he's the short one, much too short. That one is Andric – he's taller than me, but a completely uncoordinated IT nerd. Not the man for you, I promise. And for the record,' Fraser took the photo out of her hands as he spoke, 'you're really lucky you have no sisters right now,' he took the glass out of her hand and pulled her up from the table, 'plus I am seriously wishing I was an only child,' he kissed her hand, 'with only Den Jnr for competition.'

Tuula watched his gaze focus on her face and as the moment lengthened she knew he was going to kiss her. She leant in to close the gap and surrendered for a moment, but was also the first to pull away.

Fraser frowned and seemed as if he was going to say something but drew her down to the sofa instead. He must have subvocalized as the music changed and the lights dimmed, but he was still frowning, pursing his lips as if deciding how to word something.

'Tuula,' Fraser began, then stopped. A frown appeared as he started a micro debate in his head. If he asked "would she" ever steal it, it would be an indirect question: easier to lie. How to phrase it so that she can see he doesn't believe it but can also read her reaction in her face just to make sure? Impossible…

'I just need to ask you…Did you steal that ring from your father?' He asked softly, no judgement.

'What?' she almost shrieked before pacing away from him, '*this* is what you have been stewing over?' she whirled round to face him, 'You think I stole that gaudy piece of –?' words deserted her.

Fraser sighed, evading the question and physically distancing yourself from the conversation both pointed towards lies. But then enraged girlfriend body language might be similar. He smiled, was she his girlfriend? Had they ever made that clear to each other? 'That was a stupid question, I'm sorry.'

Tuula glanced up, he did look genuinely sorry. 'Stupid because you don't believe I could ever do that, or stupid to ask me right now?' she whispered.

Fraser smiled, reminded of her astuteness as ever, 'Come

here,' he smiled, opening his arms wide.

She took two reluctant steps forward, he hadn't answered the question after all, and allowed herself to be hugged without reciprocating. 'You are so infuriating,' she mumbled against his chest, 'with your bloody stupid charm hiding all your true agendas!'

'I know you wouldn't have done that.' He murmured into her hair.

Tuula sneaked her hands around his back. It was a warm, solid back. 'Well that's good, because I didn't take it.'

Fraser smiled on the inside, triumphing over his worst self, and tightened his grip around her like a shield. She had just needed his trust before she gave her answer. She needed him, even if she didn't know it yet.

8 TRIUMPH & HOPELESSNESS

'Oh for Grut's sake!' Dave swore as he slipped off the stardrive and caught his wrist on an exposed screw end. He put his wrist in his mouth and sighed at the lack of concern from either of his two flatmates.

'Dave,' Guin started, obviously taking an extended break from his current assignment, surrounded as he was with cans and shrink wrap remains, 'Do you have any idea what McTherg is doin' over by there? He has a strange expression on his face which looks like a cross between love and constipation.'

'You may be interested to know,' Therg began, his face deadpan, 'that one of our local architects has a hobby.'

'What?' enquired Dave with his wrist obscuring his words. Guin was a little less eloquent: 'You half-baked pony, what are you up to?'

Look!' Therg helped Guin to look through the telescope... with a little more force than was strictly necessary. It was focused on a drab block of flats a little to the East and was largely made up of large rectangular greyish bricks except for a slash of coloured bricks diagonally across it. 'The blue ones look random, yes?'

'I think it looks revolting.' Guin replied, grinning.

'Count in prime numbers across the bricks and each blue will score a hit.'

'Hey, cool! Like battleships for mathematicians!'

'Hng.' Therg snorted his derision. 'Any fool knows primes. But that's not it.'

'If the 'y' axis is primes, wait for this one. The 'x' axis is happies!'

'Yes Therg. Remind my peasant brain what those second set are again would you?'

'You know...happy numbers? Like 1, 7, 10, 13, 19, 23, 28, 31, 32, 44, 49? Actually ignore the last one – he didn't make the building wide enough.' Therg peered around at the two blank faces and sighed. 'A happy number is any whole number, where, when you replace the number by the sum of the squares of its digits, and repeat the process, the number equals one.'

Therg's eyes twinkled as he added, 'Did I say that slowly enough for you ponies without distinction at Zee-tech level maths? Guin, I am looking at you.'

'Pffer! Zee-tech isn't even worth the effort. You should

have done a Q module like me. Then you'd know what all-nighters are made for.'

Dave wandered off at this point and Therg found himself stuck with Guin as his only audience.

'Anyway,' he began, 'the point is that each blue brick is pinpointed by these two sequences of numbers. I think somewhere on the Lunar 17 architecture team is a frustrated numerologist. Do you want to see?'

Guin shook his head: 'I'll take your word for it, McTherg, or maybe I'll just continue in the knowledge that there is enough useless knowledge in your head to make sense out of any random nonsense!'

'How upsetting. It makes me wonder why I bother.'

It was at moments like this that Guin always wondered whether Therg was actually joking or not. His deadpan expression was unmovable.

Guin scratched the back of his head with a furrowed brow, 'I do want to know one thing... How is it you know the word numerologist in your second language?'

'Aha. Ancient Russian work ethic.' His eyes narrowed a fraction. 'And extraordinarily high IQ.'

'Yess!' Screamed Dave, punching the air, 'I just configured the 3D telescope!'

'Yeah yeah, that pile of junk has been sitting there for a year and no-one's got it to see further than a binocular 'plant.' Guin cackled near-silently in his mirth.

'Hey look!' Dave's voice accelerated in excitement, 'I've just zeroed in on Enceladus...block 3, residence 24!'

'Really? I wonder if I know anyone down there?' Guin pondered.

'What is it with you thinking you might know someone 30,000 klicks away?'

'It's a Welsh thing, bach.'

'What is this Back thing you always say, Guinevere?' Therg asked.

'Not back...bach', it's a Welsh thing as well.'

*   *   *

Amiette skulked around her bedroom. She let her feet drag and her shoulders droop and swung her shoulders from side to side in exaggerated melancholy. Even these theatrics failed to give her any satisfaction in self-indulgent wallowing. She felt very bipolar today. She could still feel the memory of yesterday's euphoria like the trails of a dream floating away. She could remember the pleasure of a job well done, the endless possibilities, the limitless potential...she just couldn't recapture any of it. Not that she wanted to recapture last weekend's row with her sister, or deciding to have a fling with the butcher.

She sat down heavily and tapped her 'plant, subvocalising to open her notes on possible triggers. She added 'heavy rain' and 'walking past cat's grave in garden'. She paused and added 'receiving bill for impulse-buy boots.' She reached over and popped two pills in to a glass. She realised it couldn't be that bad or she wouldn't still be following the doctor's orders. "Always *always* take your medicine." She mimicked out loud. Her implanted processor asked if she wanted to add this to her open note, which she declined before saving it and shutting down the file.

Her brain skittered backwards and relived the agony of embarrassment of the fumbling kisses. Why did she do that? In what universe is that okay? The mother of a grown boy, for space's sake, and what is she doing? Ruining a perfectly good acquaintance…and her only chances of getting half decent steak.

She thought about the row with her sister. Warning her to stop ringing Genilh in the middle of the night. Warning her that his grades would suffer. That he was worried about her…that he didn't need that kind of pressure. She had screamed back. Said she never wanted to speak to her again. She had said some hideous things. She had felt utterly invincible. Now it seemed reckless, insensitive and stupid.

The hollow feeling inside her stomach appeared. She wondered if it was there last night when she was lying awake. Not as active as butterflies, or as sickening as remorse. She examined the edges of her tummy with her fingertips trying to visualise the emotional void growing inside her. She didn't even want to think about it too closely. It felt too deep and empty. It had a pull of its own that could drag you in. She visualised all the flickers of positivity being pulled in by the hole and pushed beneath encrusted layers of ingrained pointlessness.

Her house was pointless. Her family was pointless. Cleaning was pointless. Her life…pointless. Nobody cared whether she was having a shitty day or not.

Genilh probably didn't even know. Why should he? He didn't live here anymore. Genilh had rung from uni yesterday – he'd been annoyed at the man next to him on the pod who had an extra wide projected screen and was tapping his non-existent keyboard mere centimetres above Genilh's own thigh.

Worse than this though, much worse, was that she didn't really care that she was having a shitty day. It was useless feeling upset about it...one way or the other, it didn't actually matter. She was a blip. A spec. Who would notice if she disappeared?

She looked out at the orange glare outside the window. She could just make out the protective hexagonal grid glinting in places like fluorescent orange peel. From her bedroom window she could see some but not all of the windows of her three neighbours whose gardens adjoined hers. They had made efforts over the years to obscure the views with various garden plants, trees and paraphernalia, but it was dome living, after all, and space was not abundant. Their house was in the biggest town of the single Titan dome. It was called Stibo: ST25A9 named after the team that came to set up the telepad, and was the first settlement built for the astronautic engineers and raw material extractors. There was still a museum in the town centre with some of the original equipment. Unfortunately Titan never took off like its icy neighbour Enceladus, being neither so picturesque nor so upmarket. Large parts of the Titan dome were places you wouldn't want to be stuck in if you missed the last pod home. And no-one had ever attempted a second dome on Titan...which speaks for itself.

Amiette watched the weather changing. It always happened

in a straight line, because no matter how random they made the weather (within certain workable parameters, that is) they hadn't found it important to residents' mental health to keep weather fronts irregular. It used to amuse Amiette watching a vertical line of rain approaching the garden from right to left. Until the day three years ago when she had watched the end of a rain pattern, seen the sparkling rain drops on the garden, and realised this was the best it was going to get. Genilh had been fifteen. She had been in the middle of a particularly long and revolting spell of depression.

Seeing the rain now gave Amiette a jolt. She did not want to be looking in to the medicine cupboard to calculate how many of this or that might be enough. Not today anyway.

She picked up a pair of pink wellies as the rest of her shoes seemed to have disappeared from the shoe rack, and she didn't trust herself enough to find another pair in case she gave up the idea of getting outside the house today. She walked quickly until the house was far enough behind her that she felt safe. She was out. She was prepared to distract her brain. She looked around her searching for inspiration. The dusty road was familiar. It led to a pod station. She would board the first pod that came along and go wherever it took her.

The first pod was a number 29. A spark of memory assailed her. She began to wonder if she had done this very thing before. When she came to a vaguely familiar wharf she got off and looked about her. Yes. Definitely familiar. She had been drawn to the cemetery because she wanted to remind herself why she didn't want to be dead, and to watch other people's misery outweigh her own. She had met a cross little lady with a squished up nose and neat grey hair.

Amiette paused at the edge of the grass. Sure enough there was the very same crazy lady. Sitting on some kind of blanket seeming to be in the middle of a full-blown row with a headstone.

She contemplated tiptoeing across or announcing her presence, but finally decided on just sitting down and waiting, but the sharp little eyes swung around and held her pinned. The old lady beckoned with a sharp motion that made Amiette wonder whether it was actually a younger woman with a mask on. A crazy younger woman with a mask on, she mentally amended. Still. She had come out to distract her brain, and what was this but distraction?

'Amiette. Hmm. Sit! Coincidence? Probably not.' Edytha talked with her eyes on the horizon. Amiette wasn't sure if she was still talking to the grave or not. But she sat down obediently, recognising a voice of authority when she heard one.

'I'm sorry to interrupt you.' She began hesitantly in a fairly colourless tone of voice, and realised it was the first time she had spoken to somebody real today. She tried harder to inject notes of enthusiasm to her speech. 'I don't know why I'm here really.' She smiled. It was a horrible effort.

'You look sick like a donkey.' Edytha returned briskly. 'Your subconscious probably brought you.' She took a deep breath and looked up to the orange atmosphere above the dome. 'Amazing thing, the subconscious. Yours is trying to help you, I would say.'

Amiette found it oddly comforting to be neither the object of pity nor annoyance. It was a relief to be just 'there'. 'I didn't recognise the stop until it wharfed. Where are we, exactly?'

'Diakon. The outskirts.' Edytha cackled. 'Not that it gets any better the further on you go. Let me introduce you to my husband.' She gestured towards the stone. 'This is, was, sorry, still can't get it, Oszkár. Oszkár, this is Amiette. There we go now. Oszkár we are going to take a walk – you won't mind.' She turned to look conspiratorially at Amiette. 'The old goat. He never could walk anyway - he'd only be moaning if he came.'

Amiette reflected on her safety a little, walking with this crazy lady who talked as if her dead husband might suddenly up and join them, and who darted little furtive glances in all directions before she moved anywhere, but either didn't care enough or needed the distraction badly enough. 'I'm afraid I forgot your name,' she said instead.

'Edytha.' Came the firm reply. 'Edytha Orlov.'

*   *   *

Fraser opened his FTs at work and saw two transmissions awaiting his attention. The first was from Varn. It was a 4th July celebratory message giving a less than spectacular digital display of fireworks across his visual field. He smiled, though the cheap graphics left a burn on his retina. When he opened the second message his pulse quickened, there had not been a theft by the dinner set gang for three months. He had no new leads and was no closer to finding the perpetrator. But it was his most interesting case. A lot of his role nowadays seemed to be managing teams, and resolving disputes, not solving crime. The FT explained the bare bones of the latest theft. It came from a DI Cralken based on Europa. Not the 23rd, where he had snuck into Blue, but LPD 22. Not quite as exclusive, but property prices effectively kept the raff and skaff out.

The FTT had a read receipt attached which Fraser duly sent back. He started a fresh FTT to DI Cralken asking to visit the scene of the crime with a view to comparing sites, and to liaise with him and his officers regarding any follow up and enquiries. About a minute later he received a stiffly worded reply. It seemed DI Cralken would of course be happy to see him in Europa if he didn't mind the expense of travelling, and would be prepared to share information already gathered, to the benefit of any LPDPF officer, as procedure allowed. He also generously offered to send holographic footage of the sites from earlier this morning, in case this was preferable to DI Moldonny actually coming in person.

Fraser smiled, the cost of travelling was always the least of his worries when it came to re-arranging his molecules. He just hoped his charm would survive intact. He sent back a friendly reply assuring him that any time he could spare would be most gratefully received, and that he always preferred to use his own senses first hand, and to expect him at 09:30, or thereabouts.

He padded to the LPDPF building on LPD 22 with a smile fixed in place, and took a deep breath while his lungs were still his own. When he felt the weight of his own body rejoin him on an almost duplicate navy telepad he expelled it quickly, 'Morning Sergeant.' He nodded to the man awaiting him.

'Morning DI Moldonny. Pleasant commute?'

'Nice to be using the Police system – less queuing! Shall I pop my head in to DI Cralken's office, or is he having a bad day?'

The sergeant had to visibly restrain a smile. 'He sent me sir, to show you around, being busy, sir. He is meeting with CO Calligan, I think.'

Fraser squinted to recall Calligan's face: a little corpulent, jolly, straight-forward...almost the antithesis of his own CO. 'Yes, I think I've met your Chief of Ops. He seems a good man. Does he make a good boss?'

'Yes, most definitely, sir. He was the right man for the job.' The sergeant stopped talking abruptly, and continued again, 'Shall I take you to the scene?'

Fraser wondered about the office politics on Europa. It would be a prestigious position as CO of any of the three Domes on this elite moon. Maybe Cralken was just bitter.

They walked down drab grey corridors and passed old and battered non-moulding seats. It felt like an institution...one that had been financially abandoned.

As the pod left the police offices he glanced back at the building he was leaving behind. The Europa splendour was more evident here, it looked striped navy and gold, but the navy came from a clever window tint and the gold was in fact a smooth creamy yellow polished stone. The base was broad with three linked towers and a central lift. It was an impressive structure, probably one of the tallest in this dome. Europans obviously cared more for the appearance of safety than the efficiency or comfort of their police force. But he guessed they wouldn't often set foot *inside* the building.

The waterway picked a delicate line through the built-up area, but it couldn't have been more than twenty minutes before they wharfed in front of a large private residence. Unlike the gilded, stuccoed, pillared magnificence that

Nollerton House aspired to, this house was sleek and modern. The holos that Fraser had been studying on the pod journey showed the house at night, or as the estate agent blurb that came with the holo stated: "The residence shown here nestled deep in the shade of Jupiter". Even without its clever up-lighting, it still appeared cool and strangely calming. There were large one-way-glass panels, and the roof looked vaguely Old Scandinavian with its slight overhang, while still managing to blend well with its neighbours.

Sergeant Wan took out a micro-key and unlocked the door. He noticed Fraser's surprise and explained as he pushed the door open. 'Mr and Mrs Catenay have given us free access all day. They've gone to their daughter's house while we investigate.'

Fraser thought back to Elbeth and Yer Catanay's initial interview following the 'Sunshine Yellow' theft back in March. He wondered which combination of characteristics the daughter may have inherited...Yer's lurch-like forehead perhaps, or Elbeth's high cheek bones and pursed lips. Now, though, he supposed he had to concede that they were less likely to be suspects for the preceding two robberies. Unless they would benefit from the insurance, he thought, or unless this was a copycat theft. He made a note sub-vocally to check the Catanay's financial situation, and then changed his mind and messaged it to Varn instead. No reason why his partner shouldn't have some work to do.

He followed the sergeant through the silent corridors and high, airy rooms until they reached the vault. It was a similar design to Mariposa Eastman's in that it had a 24 digit entry code, but the major difference, as far as Fraser could see, was that this vault appeared to be equipped to withstand the end of worlds. It was the size of a normal room, which might be considered small in this house, with 8 solid bars which would normally lock the metal door into place, but were now in their 'out' position as if the security system had been re-set. Alongside one wall of the vault were a fascinating array of guns, batons, old style crossbows and one vintage grenade. At the back of the room were a few gold framed canvasses the size of a horse. To the left was a sofa bed, table, kettle and sink unit (the paranoia of the upper classes was still rife, Fraser thought, looking at the mini panic room within the safe). Sitting on an antique piece of furniture to the right was an open briefcase, with moulded padding showing a conspicuous hole.

'No prints, sir.' Sergeant Wan volunteered before Fraser had a chance to ask. 'And all paperwork for this lot present and correct, sir.' He swept an arm over the armaments section.

Fraser nodded, but subvocalised a message to Varn to check any military contacts to the Catenays.

'The timed entry shows the robbery occurred at 5:20am this morning.' Wan continued his summary, 'Sophisticated equipment needed to open this,' he pointed towards the antique, which did have glints of metal showing that suggested it wasn't the innocent wooden structure it appeared to be, 'and possibly to ascertain which briefcase he wanted. Cralken thinks a portable scanner of some kind. We're looking at recent purchases at the moment.'

'I read this morning that there were an array of identical black cases?' Fraser looked around.

'Hmmm. Mr Catenay took the lot with him. I heard him say we could nick the paintings with his pleasure but he couldn't have anything else go astray! Maybe his daughter has another doomsday cupboard for him to hide his stuff.' Sergeant Wan didn't seem to appreciate Yer Catanay's humour. Fraser suspected Yer had probably been joking, but didn't suggest it.

Fraser paced the route of the robbery, talking to himself as he went. 'So he uses some kind of device to crack the code without harming the vault itself...and he scans this deceivingly high-tech cupboard, goes straight to this case without disturbing any of the others...and leaves this case here as I see it, while disappearing with a rather large emerald.'

'Not just any emerald, sir!' Sergeant Wan elaborates, 'it was a 1759 carat dodecahedral crystal from old Columbia, deemed most valuable on the black market because it hasn't yet been made into anything, so escaped the inter-structural micro-chipping that tracks almost all valuable jewellery. Mr Catenay was planning to sell it, he told us this morning, as his insurance wanted him to chip it or lose his cover. No leaks to the press sir, and only one very highly encrypted FTT sent to the jewellers by Mr Catenay himself, sir, that being his line of business...Encryption that is, sir. Not even his wife knew he had it. She was most put out, I can tell you, when she found out this morning.'

'So more highly expensive, highly unavailable equipment needed in the setting up of this heist.' Fraser mused. 'A scanner, an entry kit, decryption software to combat the market leaders...Interesting. Has Cralken considered a partnership?'

'Not sure sir, I don't think he's ruled anything out.'

Fraser moved the side of his index finger over his bottom

lip, the better to think, 'Any government links to the Catenays?'

'Lots sir, unfortunately. It's the kind of circles they move in.' Wan replied.

'Could you forward your info to my partner, DI Delot?'

'Pleased to, sir.' Sergeant Wan had not yet managed to prevent the slack mouth side effect of sub-vocalising, common among kids when they first get their 'plants. Poor Wan, Fraser thought, I bet he was picked on in school. No amount of ethnic identity (which would ordinarily have lifted him to super-cool status) would make up for the slack mouth.

By the time Fraser arrived back in Lunar 17 he was weary, but not so weary that he couldn't pop in and see his favourite suspect. He disliked feeling so unsure of his position with a woman. The perpetual niggling feeling that he should ring her on any pretext at all was definitely beginning to annoy him. Since their first date in April Tuula had used several excuses not to see him – his involvement in the ongoing case was her prime one, but an ice-cave exploring holiday for almost a fortnight was a close second, and working hard at the water plant followed closely behind. They had messaged each other to oblivion, but she hadn't come over since he'd asked her whether she'd stolen from her father. 'Rooky mistake!' he thought for the gazillionth time.

He subvocalised a message to Tuula telling her he would be seeing her in ten minutes, and to ask whether she was at work or home.

Tuula grimaced as she looked around her apartment –

Jaimey had enjoyed the break a little too much while she had been away with Cailly. Her table was covered with rows of perfectly flattened coca cola cans, stacked to various heights, which she was sure would have some deep and significant meaning to her Aspie half brother. It seemed likely that ten minutes of tidying might undo the good work that two weeks' solitary living had done for him. Tuula sent back '*MEET IN THE PARC?*'

'*WHICH ONE?*' Flickered across her left visual field in a pale blue font.

'*THE PARC.*' She sent back, and then: '*HOW MANY PARCS DO YOU KNOW OF ON LUNAR 17 LAWMAN?*'

She smiled when the answer flashed back: '*OH, SO WE'RE LIMITING OURSELVES TO THIS DOME ALL OF A SUDDEN ARE WE, SOCIALITE?*'

She had never been with a guy before who relentlessly ridiculed her social status. They were either a part of her own circle and therefore consistently charming but rarely mocking, or they were scared rigid of her father.

She wriggled her toes as she toyed with sending an even cheekier return, but decided she would prefer to gauge his reaction face to face. She had been away for long enough to have reassembled all the apprehension of a first date. She reapplied lip gloss, smiled at her reflection and shut the door.

Fraser jogged the last three steps towards Tuula and fell in to step beside her, linking her arm in his as he did so. Tuula nearly jumped out of her skin which made him laugh.

'You could have been anybody!' Tuula complained, though

grateful her heart had something plausible to race for.

'How many other men have you made an assignation with in this park?! You wound me. And there was me giving you ten minutes warning to hide the multitudes of men you've been seeing instead of me…Makes me wish I'd caught you by surprise.' Fraser returned with a sly smile.

Tuula stopped walking and narrowed her eyes. 'If you knew women at all you would know ten minutes is not enough to hide anything! But maybe you wanted to catch me by surprise? Are there lawmen at my flat right now digging up the bodies in the backyard?'

Fraser sighed, took her arm again and dragged her forwards. 'It's my job to ask. You should take it as the compliment it is that I don't seem to be able to stop seeking you out. If it really came to it I don't know how many of our meetings I could justify in a court of law.'

'You're a smooth talker Muldonny, you've probably got it covered. Right now I have to assume that some of this smoothness for me is to ease the exchange of information.'

'Wish I could ease the exchange of something!' Fraser muttered.

'What?'

'Nothing. Listen. Since you've reduced me to business I might as well get that part over with. He initiated his recorder and planted himself in front of her. 'You are being recorded, you've done this before so you understand the drill.'

Tuula grumped.

Fraser patiently explained in a soft voice as if he was talking to a toddler: 'You have to say you understand for the record. Remember?'

'I understand.' Tuula intoned frostily.

'Great! Were you aware your friends the Catenays were burgled in the early hours of this morning?'

'They are my parents' friends, not mine. But as it happens – yes – I was aware.'

'Can you tell me where you were at 05:20 this morning?'

'Yes, in bed.' Tuula took a deep breath to control the blush. 'My brother was in the house – he can vouch for me.'

'Great, let's go.' Fraser took her hand and started off walking again. 'Recording's finished by the way!'

'But-'

'Yup?' Fraser answered too quickly, enjoying her discomfort.

'Is this business? I mean,' she frowned, 'is this necessary?'

'Deeply necessary I'm afraid.' Fraser grinned crossing his fingers behind his back.

As they approached the front door Tuula began a halting explanation. 'Listen, my brother has been here for a while and he's not the tidiest person you'll ever meet.'

'No worries...Stop fretting.'

'I'm not fretting!'

Fraser took her finger nail and examined it. 'Nail biting says otherwise.' He kissed the tips of her fingers but immediately let them go. 'Never hide anything from your very own Lawman.'

Tuula scraped together her scattered wits as she opened the door. 'And the charm offensive is back. I missed it while I was away.' She lifted her eyebrows in challenge.

'So…too busy missing me to run off with any rugged ice climbers?' Fraser asked.

'As you see. I'm back. Minus extraneous baggage.' In fact there had been one stupidly persistent well-dressed guy. But he had been strangely unappealing.

Tuula noticed again the gleaming table top and ranked squashed cans. 'Jaimey!' She called, 'I'm home.'

'Okay.' He called back.

'I have a –' she paused, 'friend with me.' She called.

'Okay.'

'I mean, can you come in here and meet him?' She called back. She turned to Fraser, 'He's not very comfortable meeting people.'

Jaimey slunk in to the room and looked above and to the right of Fraser's head. The foot tapping increased as Fraser said Hi. He seemed to be anxious about something.

'Hi.'

'I met you at the ball didn't I?'

'Yes the Nollerton Ball. On the first of March – the third month is Tuula's favourite, did you know?'

'No, I-' Fraser began, but Jaimey was on the move.

'I have to go out now Tuula. I'll see you later, bye.'

'Hmm,' Tuula talked to the door, 'He's jittery today.' When she turned back Fraser was examining the cans. 'Don't touch those!'

'Hey?'

Tuula took the can from his hands and replaced it. 'They'll be arranged in some special way. My brother needs his stuff to be left alone...Sorry.'

'No don't worry, it's fine.'

'Oh no! You never asked him about this morning! Shall I 'path him and get him back?'

'Actually, I didn't really need to talk to him right now.'

Tuula frowned, 'So...'

Fraser interrupted: 'So why is number three your favourite?'

Tuula smiled. 'Jaimey's not the only one with some dysfunctional brain wiring.' She laughed at Fraser's expression. 'I'm allowed to take the mickey – he's my brother. And anyway, I can't talk – I have synaesthesia.'

'Say what? You have to remember to dumb it down a bit

when you talk to me, socialite.' He put a hand on either side of her hips and pulled her closer. 'Tell me... in words of one syllable.' He smiled his lazy smile.

'It basically means I feel numbers with colours. Three is a cool, fresh green like the new leaves in spring. And green is my favourite.'

'I would expect nothing less, my little robin in her tree.' He smiled. 'Tell me the others.'

'Four is a bright blue, but it sort of grows, five is pale yellow, a bit bouncy...'

Fraser laughed and leaned a little closer. 'Buying flowers for you just got a shade more tricky. I'm going to write this down – you never know when you might need it. Okay, my implant is at my disposal, tell me what six is.'

'It's embarrassing.'

Fraser lifted her chin up to look at him. 'Tell me anyway.'

'It's sort of purple, but a dangerous kind of purple, and alluring like a siren,' she whispered.

'And seven? Fraser kissed her gently, 'poor seven stuck next to wicked six all the time.'

Tuula kissed him back, almost without thinking. 'Seven is pure white like snow, almost glistening.' Fraser linked his hands in hers.

'Eight is ochre, nine is cold and dark like infinity. It's a really nasty one.' She took a step back, as if the horror of number nine had awakened her somehow.

Fraser casually got himself a drink and gave her back some personal space. 'So what's one and two? I really can't stand unfinished lists.'

Tuula marvelled at the lightening quick change from lover to joker and chastised herself yet again for getting carried away.

'One is a pulsing sort of hopeful yellowy orange...and two is red – a really simple, deep red.'

Fraser smiled. 'And you couldn't have chosen two as your favourite number?'

Tuula rested her teeth on her bottom lip, frantically wondering how serious he was. 'Nope,' she whispered.

Jaimey re-entered the flat repeating what sounded like 'Oh, oh, oh, oh, oh' with a repeating pattern of intonation, but he disappeared again without a word to anyone, giving Fraser the impression he wasn't bright enough to stay out long enough to make sure his leaving looked genuine. He admired his Robin-bird even more for what he assumed must have been a lifetime of duty and caring.

Tuula saw that Fraser was hovering and decided to play a dangerous card, 'So, are you staying to eat?'

'Yeah' His lightening grin returned, 'Thought you'd never ask!' He patted his slim stomach fondly, 'you know you can't ever hope to feed me enough.'

Fraser plonked himself on a stool the better to watch her flit around the small kitchen. His eyes slid from her narrow waist to various objects in the room and back to her, until an interesting round object caught his eye. 'What *is* that?'

'What?' Tuula answered, turning from a sizzling pan to follow the line of his outstretched hand.

'That round ended wooden thing?' He tried not to visualise the dimensions of the mark on the …. Tuula was *not* a suspect.

'It's a pestle! Don't you have one?'

'Not only do I not have one, I don't even know what one is!'

'It's for grinding stuff – spices and garlic and whatnot…how do you do your garlic, then?'

'Us farm boys squash garlic with the back of a spoon.' Fraser let his dead pan expression slip a little, 'that or our bare hands.'

'Ha ha,' Tuula spoke out the words.

'So are they common those pestle things, amongst the rich and famous of the galaxy?'

Fraser caught the rising flush and stopped himself from speculating. She was just noticing the rich comment, not hiding a guilty conscience. Her profile didn't fit anyway. 'Ten a penny amongst the nobility, pestles are. Maybe I'll buy you one.'

Tuula smiled shyly, and Fraser forgot case details in the lure of future gifts with his brave little robin.

Fraser was happy to drink expensive wine, eat cheap food, tease his girl about roughing it only in part, and settle down in front of a film.

Half way through Tuula tucked her legs up on the sofa and Fraser lifted his arm so she could nestle her head into his chest. The film flickered on to its end, and Fraser dropped his head to rest on top of hers. She seemed almost asleep. Her breathing was slow and even. He kissed the top of her hair: slowly and very gently.

Tuula felt a wave of goosebumps rise from her stomach to her throat. She had to remind herself to breathe. He probably thought she was sleeping. She wouldn't ruin the moment. She screwed her eyes tight shut, and stayed that way until Fraser's arm went dead and he slid it out ungraciously and shook it with his other hand.

Jaimey was still jittery the following morning. His 'Oh' mantra continued as he made drinks and padded round the flat with socks but no shoes. He wore socks with toes and had to wear colours that matched the days of the week.

'Are you okay Jai?'

'Okay. Jai. That rhymes.' Jaimey replied abstractedly without answering the question. He was arranging cans again with a wiping and rewiping ritual that seemed to last longer today.

'Aspie! Everything alright at work?' Tuula tried a different tack.

'No! Ozzy won't reply to my FTTs. What's the point in having business contacts if they don't reply?'

Tuula was well versed in Jaimey's frustrations when other adults were not on the 'same page' as he was at any given moment of the day.

'He's probably just doing something else and hasn't had a chance to reply. Why don't you work on something else and come back to that later?'

'It needs to be now!' Jaimey replied, jiggling his foot in turmoil.

Tuula remembered one particularly awful afternoon when Jaimey had been twelve and she was six or seven. He was visiting Herve for the weekend and Saphie had obviously had a slow week as she had been 'updating' the house. Jaimey had taken exception to her perfume, her food, her plans for the day and the changes she had made to the guest bedroom he had always slept in. Jaimey did not do change fantastically well. Although, to be fair, dealing with Saphie had to be difficult for anyone. Saphie ended up shrieking and Jaimey broke several things in his room before ending up with his hands pressed tight over his ears, rocking on the floor. Tuula remembered disobeying her mother for the first time that day and creeping into his room. She had sat next to him until he was breathing normally and then asked him what he was doing. Jaimey actually liked straightforward questions without any emotions to cloud them, like accusation or anger. As the years rolled by Tuula had found more and more that she preferred talking to her step brother than her emotionally-charged mother. Tuula and Jaimey shared a love of numbers. She had taught him how to reduce his anxiety by focusing on his favourite ones. She had even coloured in a few at school and brought them home for him. He used to hang his favourites up in his room and trace them with his fingers when he was most stressed (apart from the times Saphie decided to 'improve' his space). Come to think of it… she hadn't seen any up lately… maybe that was a sign his latest therapy was working.

9 WISDOM

Tad trudged the familiar route from his wharf to home. He was alone by choice. He had peeled off from Frel and the others early to save them the trouble of dumping him and talking about all the exciting things they were going to do together. It didn't matter anyway. Today was the day his new score card came out. His dad would finally see his maths score on the FTT and be proud of him. Then maybe his mum and dad would stop having so many silences together. He had noticed the silences more and more lately. And then extra loud conversations about weird things when he walked in the room.

He turned the corner and scrambled through the door hardly daring to smile so he didn't give away the A he knew was hiding in the score transmission like a glowing beacon of happiness for his whole family.

But no-one awaited him in the kitchen with proud smiles and arms extended waiting to give him a hug. He could hear a hushed and fast conversation coming from his mum's study.

'Mum did you see my -?' Tad began, bursting through the door.

'Not now Tadelesh!' Bracq uttered harshly.

'Why don't you go get a drink Tad?' Ymarise turned to Tad without remembering to wipe the worried expression from her face, 'I have to talk to Dad for a bit, okay?'

'What's the matter?' Tad asked, a slight wobble in his voice betraying him only slightly.

'Everything's fine sweetheart. Your Dad just had some news from work that we need to discuss.'

'Now please Tad!' Bracq lifted his eyebrows and indicated the door.

Tad walked to the kitchen, took his shoes off and came straight back to the office on tiptoe. He heard snatches of conversation: 'We need to go through the finances…We need to look at the worst case scenario…Well let's not assume it will come to that Bracq…When shall we tell Tad?...No, I know…Yes, it might mean that…I don't know…He'll understand Bracq, I know it…You'll find another job…No, I do realise that it's just-…Yeah…'

Tad heard footsteps approaching and ran upstairs, ignoring the thirst in his throat and the different kind of burn in his chest. The kind of burn that feels like a hole and a weight all at once.

Tad counted the times the office door opened and closed.

He counted the number of times the boiled water unit issued water to make drinks. He counted all the peas on his plate of dinner that his mum brought to him in his room as a special treat, but he didn't eat all of the rabbit burger or the sweet potato waffles.

He thought of the shining A that still lay hidden in the FTT from school and wondered if it might still magically solve his parents' problems, but he didn't risk going downstairs.

As he brushed his teeth he imagined how his dad would look if he would just read his maths scores, and wiped at his eyes as well as his mouth with the towel when he finished, ignoring the warmth behind his eyelids.

He heard the front door open and slam shut from his bed in the darkness and noticed the time. No one ever went out at this time on a school night. Not even for the twice a year university dinner…and then there was always a nice babysitter who let him eat toffees in bed.

Bracq quickened his pace as he walked away from the dark house. He just needed some thinking time…some breathing space. He needed some time to wrap his brain around it so he could figure out what to think and how to feel. He didn't like knowing that others were trying to reassure him: it felt like it was another male role he was being denied.

He walked in the chilly night air trying to let the deep lungfuls soothe his overwrought brain. He jumped on a late pod and got off it at the next stop when he realised sitting still was definitely not helping. Further ahead some lights gleamed in orange and two shades of blue. As he drew closer the lights became more distinct until he saw two familiar shops: one a Gillette Hair Stylist, obviously closing for the night, the other a Casino Royale, with two unattractive clients hovering outside in deep conversation, and the 'e' missing from the end of the name.

A man and a woman locked the Gillette door and ignored him as they hunched into their coats and went their separate ways.

Bracq sat on the ledge of the Gillette window. It was too narrow for comfortable sitting, which suited his mood, but every few minutes he had to readjust his position to keep from sliding off completely.

A pop-up appeared in his 'plant screen advertising male haircuts using the latest 3D techniques. Normally he would add it to his list of junk sites, but he closed his eyes and listened to the voice describing the history of the company, hoping to silence his own thoughts. He happened to know Gillette were hoping to further diversify into the leisure complex industry to compete with Interstellar Parcs. He almost hoped they would rise up and squash his soon-to-be former employer, but a small part of his rational brain remembered he didn't like their invasive marketing. They were certainly a successful company, having reinvented themselves when the problem of unwanted hair had been solved. Maybe they would be hiring new staff. If only he could line up a new job before the old one finished. If only he could find a job with an equal wage.

He must think of the bottom line. Everything would be manageable if they could keep the house. He could suffer any job if it kept them from sinking financially. Any indignity was worth the happiness of his family. Wasn't it? After all, he'd chosen to become a father. These were the consequences of his own life choices.

The Gillette pop-up faded but an icon for 10 free credits to spend in Casino Royale appeared in the top left of the screen in its stead.

Gambling wouldn't solve his problems. A small voice told him it wouldn't hurt to spend free credit. If he won and kept winning he wouldn't lose anything. He found his feet moving before he had fully decided what to do. He placed the collar of his coat next to the number 26 and watched as it was sucked away to the cloakroom. The number 26 appeared in his view with tiny red and black stripes. His heart was hammering with excitement. What if this was his lucky break? What if this was the day that changed everything?

'Place your bets!' Announced the roulette table. In reality all the equipment was crammed in, but if you just concentrated on your own screen the augmented reality created a casino hall of luscious proportions.

'Ten credits on black 26 please.' Bracq replied, thinking ahead fast. If he won this he would take it as a divine sign that his GGP involved him gambling back his good fortune and getting his life back. He would take his winnings each time and bet half of it again to reduce the risk of running out of money. He smiled and felt a fine sweat break out on his back as he watched the ball rolling around the very edge and then start to bounce. It jumped across three numbered squares and finished so quickly that he couldn't even see where red 26 had got to before it was resting in the well of black 11.

He could feel a coldness where moments ago his whole body was flushed with excitement. What a phenomenally idiotic idea. What a pitiful specimen of humanity he was to be sucked into the idea of gambling to solve a problem.

False hope was the bitterest of friends. Thank the stars he'd not wasted his own family's credit. He felt a little sick at the thought. Bracq turned and walked straight out, pulling his coat from the 26 slot as he went.

He tapped his 'plant and bought a lottery ticket instead. No harm done.

Jaimey rolled over in bed and flicked off his alarm. 7:28. He took his meds at 7:30. He had an overwhelming urge to not be alone. He walked into Tuula's room and hovered near her head. The rule was he couldn't wake anyone up before ten on a non-work day and eight on a work day. It was quarter to eight now. Tuula always told him to remember that he had to try extra hard to control his impulses until twenty minutes after the first dose of medicine because it wouldn't work until then. Was this an impulse to wake his sister up before eight o'clock or a considered decision? It was very hard to tell. 7:49. He had spent four minutes considering it. Plus Tuula was usually happy to see him. Not everyone was. He nodded his head, with a slightly harder emphasis on the forwards than the backwards. Sometimes the movement helped him think more clearly.

'Morning'. Tuula spoke groggily, opening one eye slowly, sensing the looming presence even from the depths of her unconscious state.

'Did you wake up on your own?' Jamey asked, somewhat worried as it was only 7:52. He stopped nodding his head and started tapping a finger on the side of the bed.

'Sort of.' Tuula replied, still half asleep.

Jaimey really hated vague answers. Surely everyone knew

their own minds? Had he woken her up or had she woken up on her own? The tapping increased.

Tuula came fully awake and sat up. The light came on automatically as she did so and Jaimey cringed away from it. She inspected her brother's face. There were rings under his eyes.

'Are you okay Aspie? Did you sleep okay?'

Jaimey considered his reply. 'Did you sleep okay?' he parroted, still tapping his finger.

Tuula remembered belatedly not to stack up more than one question: he didn't like it. 'Not too bad Jai. Do you want breakfast?'

'No. Thank you. I'm going to do some work.' Jaimey thought he had wanted to talk to Tuula but he decided actually her voice was too loud.

'I thought you told me you weren't working today?'

'I'm working on a project today. Projects that I enjoy outside of work are important.' He ambled out of the door.

*   *   *

Fraser looked at his screen and flicked through the details of the three heists again. Ciegham was not pleased at the idea of a 'gang' (dinnerset or otherwise) at large amongst the rich and famous with access to expensive and hard to source equipment. As he had patiently explained to Fraser the day before: all citizens needed protection, but rich citizens needed protection to such a degree as to occasionally be willing to part with their money to fund various new schemes.

Varn sauntered into his office in the LPDPF 17 building. 'How are you my friend? I was going to send my report but then I thought I would see if I had beaten you for once now that you are juggling so many pies, hmm?'

'That would be juggling too many balls, or fingers in too many pies, Varn. And either way I guess you're right. My balls and pies are too numerous, and I'm way behind on paperwork.'

Varn tilted his head a fraction, 'This is new job balls or new girlfriend pies?'

'Both probably. But I'm not sure we have an official term yet. So don't call her my girlfriend when you meet her okay?'

'If I ever get to meet this girl I will kiss her hand for being willing to take on such a case as yourself, and then I will question her with all my charm and discover all her feelings for you. Exactement! Then there will be no doubt which 'term' you use, my friend.'

Fraser sighed but with a smile, 'And you wonder why you haven't met her yet?'

'I think it is because you realise my superior style and… 'je ne sais quoi' are very appealing to a woman and you feel…ah…what is the word?'

'Happy?' Fraser tried, 'Content? Completely at ease?...Not at all intimidated or threatened?'

'Threatened! Oui, c'est ca! You are feeling *threatened* I will be whisking her off her legs!'

'Off her feet.' Fraser corrected with a chuckle. Sometimes he was sure his partner mixed his metaphors on purpose.

'DELOT!' Ciegham yelled from the corridor. 'The girl from Harbour Street is here!'

Varn winced and groaned as he stood up. 'That is my next job.' He turned back at the door and sighed 'I think I preferred it when you were plain old DI Moldonny. There is so much more walking now that I 'ave to do.'

'You might work off that paunch Varn!' Fraser replied.

'DELOT, where are you?' Ciegham shouted again.

'Give a kiss to your girl for me.' Varn shouted as he strolled out the office, not overly concerned by their enraged boss.

Fraser looked again at the screen and decided on another good old fashioned policing technique. He opened a cupboard and wheeled out a white board. It was a relic that he refused to throw away. He liked to make physical marks once in a while. It seemed to help his brain engage.

He wrote down:

1: Sunshine Yellow, Nollorton House, New Manhattan (LPD 23), Europa 6:00am 1/3 (2437)
2: Lovers Locked Ruby, Chateaux de Loire, Encaladus, 6:50am, 2/4 (2437)
3: Uncut emerald, Santark House, LPD 22, Europa, 5:20am, 4/7 (2437)

Then he added Mariposa Eastman to number 1, Saussays to number 2 and Catenays to number 3. He stepped back and looked at the information, then added the equipment and names of leads to each theft number. Finally he wrote Interplanetary Dinner Set Gang across the top, and sat down again.

A message pinged up reminding him to find green flowers for Tuula. Green for her favourite number three. He looked at the board again. A sinking feeling settled in his stomach as he flipped through Tuula's colour list and matched it against the board in front of him. Theft number one was a yellow/orange diamond and he had written warm yellow for number 1. The second theft was a ruby and he had written deep red next to Tuula's 2. The third theft was an emerald, not really a cool fresh green as he had written – more of a dark green. Surely it was a coincidence? It was just three numbers, wasn't it, in an infinitely random universe? He tried to reason with his whirling logic. He was a good judge of character. There was no way he could be so wrong. Dating a criminal? How much did he really like this girl anyway? Couldn't he just walk away now and be done? He rested his chin in his hands. No, impossible. So what then? He really liked her. The idea was ridiculous. Since when did grown men fall for a girl after three dates anyway? He liked her that's all. Liked her in a casual, offhand kind of way. She wasn't the kind of girl he would settle down with. She'd marry a Brandforth or a Litton-Strackey. Actually, no not those two, he couldn't picture her with either of them: she wouldn't settle for them anyway.

He got up and walked backwards and forwards past the board. She didn't even fit the profile – she had no connections with anyone that could get her military equipment to pull off jobs like these. She had iron alibis for two out of three of the thefts. He should know, he was one of them!

He sat down heavily on the edge of his desk and initiated a search for large blue gems, and then separately searched for sapphires, lapis lazuli, topaz and quantum quattro but there were too many to look at. He cross referenced the list with all attendees at each event and other known leads but there were still no correlations. He let out a breath he hadn't realised he was holding.

Still, he narrowed the blue gem search to those estimated at 500,000 credits and over. The top three gave further reassurance. The first has been lost for centuries, the second was held in a secure museum on Earth, and the third privately owned by a Miss Langevin. No connections to Saussay to be found.

Fraser subvocalized a message to one of his friends from the Mountford West Academy, Arno the 'Bear' Larsin.

'ARE YOU FREE TO DO ME A PERSONAL FAVOUR?'

The response was immediate:

'I'M AT HEADQUARTERS. WHAT'S UP?'

'I COULD DO WITH A C22.' Fraser replied, indicating the latest bugging device.

'WHY'S THAT PERSONAL? CAN'T YOU REQUISITION IT?'

'IT'S A BIT OFF THE BOOK.' Fraser sent back with a grimace.

'AH, CONSIDER IT DONE. NICE TO SEE YOU ENGAGING WITH A BIT OF MODERN TECH FRASER. YOU STILL AT 17?'

'YUP.' Fraser sighed, his penchant for physical rather than technological methods had earned him the nickname of Fraser 'the Relic' Moldonny back in the day. Not that he'd want to be a bear either.

'YOU MIGHT WANT TO GO WAIT BY YOUR PAD THEN.'

'WILL DO, CHEERS MATE.'

'BY THE WAY – WE NEED TO CATCH UP SOMETIME...YOU CAN TELL ME ALL ABOUT HER.'

'WHAT??' Fraser sent back, wondering if he was the one being bugged.

'IF IT'S SERIOUS ENOUGH FOR A C22, IT'S SERIOUS...'

The 'Bear' sent an exploding grin spliced with a vintage woody the woodpecker laugh.

Fraser smiled as he jogged down the corridor to his own personal nemesis, happy that he would be keeping his own molecules for today.

As he bent down to pick up the small box he caught the eye of Varn coming out of the interrogation room.

He lifted his eyebrows but drew an invisible zip over his lips. It paid to have good friends in the Force.

'Just heading out Varn – won't be long.'

'You call me if you need back up, no?' Varn smiled, then added, 'And I'll be sure to dispatch some eager young recruit who can keep up with your big legs.'

Fraser snorted: 'Me and my big legs will be just fine thanks.

See you in a few.'

He jogged out the door suddenly brimming with energy, and chose the quickest way to Tuula's flat which involved a short walk, or run, in this case, one clockwise pod and a tangle of paths to burn up some more of his adrenaline. He still found it amusing that their entire transport system still used the old terms Rimwise and Parcwise as well as Clockwise and Anticlockwise to describe the pod lines. He found it difficult to imagine the time when the dome had a parc at the centre, a shopping mall and a padding station and nothing much else.

He stopped around the corner from Tuula's flat and opened the box. He scanned the patch ID with his plant and while the programme was uploading he unwrapped the bug. It was literally bug-shaped. A small bluebottle to be exact. As it came into contact with the light it hovered out of the box about five centimetres up. The dialogue box showing a percentage download bar in his vision changed to a view from the bug. He initiated lift, trying not to move his head as if it were a giant joystick, and used his eyes to direct the flight. He landed on the window sill outside Tuula's flat after ten aborted attempts. There were no windows open. He would probably get decent readings from here, and to be honest, his directing skills were probably not up to flying in through the door in the split second someone went in. It had been hard enough to land on the ledge, and if anyone had been watching it would have looked like very erratic bluebottle behaviour.

He added all the keywords he wanted to flag up and left the C22 programme running in the background without obscuring his vision. He could look at any highlighted segments later.

*   *   *

'Guinevere *what* are you doing?' Asked Therg for the third time.

'Hnng?' Guin replied, scribbling numbers and re-scribbling when he made a mistake.

'You know, your lines are all wonky? I don't know how you can work in such a haphazard way.' Therg replied without asking his question again.

'He's right, Guin.' Dave chipped in, looking over his shoulder. 'It's like spaghetti on a page, your workings out.'

'Hold on…Be right with you…'

Dave and Therg looked at each other in puzzlement. Guin was the least likely to get caught up in his work as he enjoyed talking so very much.

'There!' He declared, throwing down a pencil and tapping his 'plant to shut it down. 'I predict a coronal mass ejection hitting our dome, disrupting the sector 5 power supply and causing a major emergency event. And when I have eaten some beans on toast I challenge anyone here to prove me wrong!'

Therg frowned. 'I am fairly certain you cannot predict a major disaster and then go and eat beans on toast. It is clearly not done.'

Dave nodded vehemently. 'McTherg is in the right of it. Watch any film! Nobody discovers a major plot point and then sits down to eat. And beans? It would be edited out at best.'

Guin prepared his meal with careful consideration. 'They never bloody eat in those films! Did you know in Die Tomorrow, Mark Housel didn't eat for 42 hours straight? I'd be dead. Actually, no. I don't think I'd be that heroic, I think I'd just faint, and that would ruin the entire scene. What would happen let me ask you, if I go charging up to the steps of the town hall and faint half way up? I'll tell you what, a mass ejection will cause all kind of trouble and I'll be stuck in hospital, that's what! I've been checking those numbers for three hours and I'm bloody smacking famished!'

Therg sat down next to him and stole a slice of toast. 'You make a fine point as always young Guin. I will eat with you to prepare myself for the gruelling hours ahead where I do indeed prove you wrong.'

'Ah fine then.' Dave said, sitting down opposite, 'we'll eat first and then we'll check the maths. Got any spare?'

Guin pushed a plate across the table with two slices piled high with virulent orange beans. 'Don't I always, bach?'

Fraser saw the nudge in his peripheral vision. The C22 bug off screen to the right was pulsing red. He maximised it, kicking up his feet on to his desk as he did so, and scrolled down the information. It was not conversation but a transmission the bug had intercepted and copied. The FTT was only two lines long. 'Oz. Need your feedback on security. Can't wait any longer. The time and day are already set. Send me details by return or my job gets exceedingly more difficult!'

Fraser felt his whole stomach and intestines sink, like his internal organs had been filled with mud. His heart thudded and his breathing quickened. He scrambled around his brain for an explanation that did not point towards the obvious. A mix up? A perfectly innocent message that he was interpreting differently because he was on a case? Some kind of mad game? Impossible. A trick? Had she found the bug and was testing him? Unlikely. Her handicapped brother? He sighed, realising he was clutching at straws. Someone was obviously trying to frame her! Or frame her brother? The step mother certainly wasn't happy with Jaimey right now. It had to be a frame of some kind. The other option was unthinkable. He breathed easier to know the C22 was off the books. No-one knew about this but him. He just had to find the real culprits and pull together enough real evidence to make it stick.

Dave rubbed his eyes one more time. 'I really think it's going to happen. We checked everything.'

Guin mumbled. He had emptied an entire bag of chocolate into his mouth and was not capable of coherent speech.

'What's that?'

'Hmm mmm...mmm MMM mmm Hng!' Guin said rolling his eyes.

'Chocolate will not help you develop your brain power Guinevere,' Therg remonstrated, 'a good bit of turnip is what you need.'

'Therg, shush, I believe the boy is trying to communicate!' Dave grinned.

'I said, of course it is!' Guin muttered, still picking chewy chocolate from his teeth. 'Maths never lies. Except statistics, obviously.'

Dave smacked Therg on the back. 'You'd better call the LPDPF McTherg – they'll listen to you.'

'What?' Spluttered Guin, 'It's my discovery Dave, I should ring!'

'No can do,' Dave explained 'Therg's got that Von-Hering thing going on. People believe him. You've got a Welsh thing going on. Russian ancestry versus welsh – you can argue with the prejudice all day long but you can't deny it's there. If you ring they'll like you, sure, but will they believe you? It's pretty crazy, as ideas go.'

'Fine – let him do it' Guin harrumphed.

'I promise you all future glory will be proportioned in an appropriate manner.' Therg answered with a twinkle in his eye.

Guin and Dave watched as Therg politely described the predicted disruption of the power source to the Guillaume Memorial Museum and the rest of sector 5, on the evening of a large public event, which would almost certainly result in the iconic 20 metre 'Impossible' sculpture outside the shopping mall, causing it to fall into the entrance hall and upper floor of the museum.

They watched as he paced the floor and patiently explained the plotting of CME's, solar winds and their density and velocity. To experienced eyes such as Dave and Guin's, the particular set of his jaw within his gaunt face indicated a growing anger with the person to whom he was attempting to communicate their important find.

He sighed as if to cleanse himself of stupidity as he tapped under the shadow of his considerable cheekbone. 'She says she will relay it to the museum but wishes to assure us that the fail-safes in place are rigorously tested for all kinds of "solar phenomenon"'.

'Hah!' Guin ejected. 'As if we hadn't checked the schematics for the Impossible's anti-gravity system. Who does she think we are…amateurs?'

'Well, strictly speaking Guin-' Dave started.

'Don't say it!'

Therg walked back into the room. 'I can't get hold of my father. I thought we could exert some of his authority. I think there's only one thing for it…'

'Please don't say my mum's authority, because then we really are lost.' Guin muttered.

'I don't think knowing every family rimwise of the finance district is the kind of authority we need.' Dave answered in a whisper.

'We must protest in person.' Therg announced.

'If I was in a film we'd have a line of black pods here by now to take us to the central pad, from where we would be transported out of harm's way to coordinate our rescue efforts with equal efficiency and modesty.' Dave quipped.

'I'll just bring some cookies for the road.' Guin scrambled under a pile of clothes and found a box which he tucked into a bag before declaring himself ready to go.

'You are not going to be allowed to play yourself in this movie!' Dave pointed out.

'Where's the harm in a bit to eat on the way?'

Therg raised an eyebrow. 'I'm out the door already whenever you two are finished?'

'Fine, fine! I'm out already! It's only my flat. Never mind me.' Dave muttered his way down the stairs and out to the path which passed several other high rises before arriving at the pod stop. As they sat on the pod in polite silence he could just make out the Conservation Park way off to the right. The leaves of the giant gnoccis tree were flaming a brilliant red, one of the Park's summer attractions. Therg sat next to him sporting a striped shirt in various shades of black with the occasional line of blood red stitching for light relief, and black trousers. He did not dress for summer well. In fact, it was quite an honour that he had deemed it worthy of going outside in broad sunlight at all. He nudged him on the elbow 'Tell Guin to give me a cookie.'

'Oh, so now he wants a cookie.' Guin dug out the box with ill-concealed pride.

They crossed the outskirts of the Interstellar Parc to the first line and caught a pod rimwards to the LPDPF. Happily there was a wharf stop just outside the ugly angular building.

'Guess the steps.' Guin started a game, well-known to all three.

'Mine, just for clarity, and to the exact point we stand at reception.' Dave added.

'Does anyone want to declare prior knowledge?' Guin continued the ritual.

'Nope?' Dave asked, 'Well in that case I'm going with…48.'

'No, way off! It's got to be 63 at least. Especially if the reception is directly in front of what looks like a lift shaft over there.'

'Could be,' Dave agreed, 'darkened glass: it's hard to tell.

Therg looked away from his serious contemplation of the short distance from where they stood to the building, 'It will be 66 to the nearest 8.'

'Sixty three, sixty four… sixty five! How does he do that? Every time? It's uncanny!' Guin exclaimed.

'It's a bit creepy, really.' Dave grumped, never a happy loser. He swiped his barcode at the empty reception desk.

'Canny is a funny word isn't it?' Therg mused. 'Canny, canny, canny. Like a scot.'

'What's a Scot?' Asked Dave.

'You ignorant pony. Have I taught you nothing?' Guin looked affronted. 'Only one of the other great Celtic nations. People whose very blood calls them to arms, to bravery, to stand knee deep in the boggy plains and shake their fists at the skies!'

'I don't even want to know what a boggy plain is.' Dave

grinned.

'I'll have you –'

'Can I help you gentlemen?' A uniformed officer arrived at the reception area, with an extra breezy tone, presumably to make up for how long it took her to get there.

'Yes we have come to report a...an adverse event.' Guin declared.

'What is the nature of your, ah, adverse event, and how is it that you came to know of it?' The officer questioned, sighing as she tucked her short hair behind one ear.

Fraser sauntered through reception and nodded to Jourdaine who seemed to be surrounded by an odd assortment of students. She threw him a harassed glare as he passed. They were all talking at once but it seemed they had forecast the next apocalypse.

'Varn's not busy if these three need interviewing?' Fraser whistled a tune and tried to contain his glee as he left the building.

*   *   *

Amiette snapped her eyes open and felt immediately alert and awake. She turned her head with precision and switched her display on to see the time illuminated in red. The display wobbled for a second then settled again to read 4:39 am. She felt so truly comfortable it felt like pure joy.

She tucked her foot into a fold of duvet, enveloped like a mollusc, and suddenly her ankle knew complete contentment. She felt giddy with excitement that she was lying there enjoying extra hours of living while everyone around her was wasting their life sleeping. She could see the faint lights on the corners of the properties adjacent to hers, and delighted in their twinkling patterns. She slid her foot up and down, feeling the bobbles on the well washed sheet.

She giggled to herself as the distant cockerel crowed its first of the day, announcing the awakening of one of her further neighbours: John the urban farmer. Lazy John! Only just waking up now!

Today would be a day of useful things! Getting things done! A day to flex flabby muscles and blow the cobwebs out of her house! She stopped as an errant memory slid in to give her a moment's pause. What was it that therapist had said, something like a RAPPER knows how to pace their activities? She scrunched one eye and looked up to the ceiling in concentrated memory retrieval...the old fashioned way - with grey matter. Her early psychiatric history was supposed to have precluded her from having any kind of internal tech. It was one of the exceptions to the insurance policy if anything went wrong with your surgery. But she had done it anyway: a moment of gay abandon, a daycase procedure and just over a thousand credits later, she was just like everyone else...sort of.

She changed her internal clock from uncompromising red back to peaceful blue

She could always access her FTTs to find the relevant therapy notes, they always send a transmission after each session as a reminder...but that felt like cheating.

It was definitely some kind of mnemonic: something like R for Rest, A to Ask for help, P for Plan, P for Prioritise, E for - she stopped, her memory suddenly stymied...eggs on toast? She smiled, eggs on toast would help anyone get through a monstrous day of tidying and sorting. She decided to start with the E and get around to the others later.

As the eggs sizzled and spat, her eyes turned to the growing piles of bills on the kitchen counter. That would be her first job. But then again, she paused. Something about the towering pile of paper gave her an internal shudder. She remembered a time when a stack of bills just like this one had marked the start of a down turn into a bleak depression. Maybe the sorting could wait. No need to tempt fate, when she was feeling so happy.

Maybe she would go shopping, not on her own - she had promised Genilh she would never do more than a food shop on her own. What she needed was someone austere to help guard her funds. She needed the opposite of reckless. Someone old and wise and –

'Bruce!' She addressed her home control unit, 'Send a message to Edytha Orlov: "Would you like to go shopping today?"' Bruce was ominously silent for a minute. He was named Bruce by Genilh after he had studied Roald Dahl at school and thought Bruce Bogtrotter, with the sole qualification of being able to eat an entire giant chocolate cake, would be easily able to run a house and manage two people's lives. Just lately Amiette had taken to talking to Bruce more than was strictly necessary. She could easily have subvocalised a message herself, but somehow, speaking aloud made her feel less lonely.

Bruce replied smoothly, with only a very slight catch in the cadence of his speech: 'Reply from Edytha Orlov: Yes, I suppose I could shop today. Where were you thinking of? What time do you want to meet?'

Amiette pondered. It had been a while since she had been in this decision making mode. Well, that wasn't strictly true. She decided to get up every day. (Well, mostly every day.) She decided lots of little things. But it was surprising to realise that she can't have done much deciding for herself and Genilh for a long time. She thought back to the times when he had run back in for her sunglasses or some other trivial thing she had forgotten, to all the times he used his own credit and then transferred funds around later, to the many times he had scrutinised pod timetables on his 'plant and ushered her on to the correct one.

'Bru-uce!' She sing-songed with renewed vigour. 'Tell Edytha: I just wanted to wander around Stibo and have a browse. Do you want to meet at nine? By the central tree? Or at the pod station? Or do you need to shop for food?'

Bruce answered almost immediately: Reply from Edytha Orlov: I know the central tree. I'll be there just before nine. There's only two pods every hour from Diakon. I don't need food, mine is delivered or grown. Is there a special reason why you are awake at six in the morning?'

Amiette glanced up and left and saw to her horror that it was a little early to be messaging, or arranging social outings. She tapped her 'plant for a speedier response, and subvocalised quickly: *'OH, NO! I'M SO SORRY. I WOKE UP EARLY AND FORGOT TO KEEP AN EYE ON THE TIME. WHY DIDN'T YOU SAY? WERE YOU ASLEEP?'*

'NO, HARDLY SLEEP AT ALL THESE DAYS. I'VE BEEN IN THE GARDEN FOR AN HOUR. IF I'D KNOWN YOU SHARED MY ABSURD DIURNAL RHYTHMS, I MIGHT BE SAVED AN

ACHING BACK RIGHT NOW.'

Amiette blushed, and was glad Edytha wasn't there to see it. She never knew whether the severe things Edytha said stemmed from real grumpiness or an acerbic sense of humour.

'SEE YOU AT THE TREE THEN. THANKS FOR COMING WITH ME.'

Amiette realised she had too much time to fill before her outing, so determined on making a start on the garden. Edytha and Urban-Farmer-John had inspired her. She spent a happy time digging, weeding, and planting seeds in sun-warmed compost 'plus' ("If you live on Titan just like us, you'll know it won't grow better than in compost plus!" was a jingle that was hard to forget).

'Who says basil won't like the quality of light on Titan? Living in Saturn's shadow never bothered the marigolds!' Amiette thought defiantly. Maybe she would be the first to grow successful basil from seed here. Maybe she would be famous.

She was so happy in her industrious early morning commune with nature that the last twenty minutes were a manic rush, and she barely had chance to scrub the dirt out of her fingernails, grab an apple and run to the station. The noise to signal the pod door closure was sounding as she sprinted up the wharf. She sat down with a sigh, in time to hear the soft whoosh of the doors closing, and grinned sheepishly at the calm travellers around her.

The low murmur of conversation around Amiette was vaguely irritating. She wanted people to speak as if they meant what they were saying! 'Speak! Be profound! Don't mumble pleasantries!' She found herself thinking. Her therapist had taught her, not long ago, that when she started to insult people directly in her thoughts it could be a sign of unreasonable irritation brought on by mania. She shut her mouth tightly, hoping to hold back the tirade. 'How funny.' She thought. 'It doesn't feel unreasonable or illogical. And they can't hear me anyway so what should it matter?'

'Idiotic, middle class, non-descript twits!' She screamed in her head, and smiled. That was the last one, she promised herself, and zipped her lips tightly shut.

As she debarked from the pod she could hear the throaty alarm of a pigeon disturbed, and wondered how the slow approach of the water-bound vessel could be in any way upsetting. She cut across the square in part to get away from the idiots she had just shared a compartment with, and partly because she felt the need to break the mould. She felt the flick of dry grass on her suddenly itchy shins, and reasoned that it was probably her karma for shouting at random people from inside her head. When she got as far as the central tree: the oldest and widest in the dome, she sat down on the artistically formed silver seating around the trunk and admired the pleasantly intrusive ticker of grasshoppers. She wasn't sitting long before the orange glare of the sun was obscured by a small and wide shadow.

'Oh hi!' Amiette responded, looking up. 'I didn't see you. Were you here already?'

'Yes, just around the corner.' Edytha spoke softly and quickly.

Amiette voiced her confusion, 'Were you really? I walked all around the tree before I sat down. I really didn't see you.'

'Hmmm. Aren't you the observant one today. Last time we met you barely saw floor under your feet! It's habit I guess.'

Amiette frowned, but shrugged off her inability to understand half of what came out of Edytha's mouth. In some ways it was a relief to be around someone crazier than she was. 'That's the trouble with being friends with me...you never know if you're going to get Jekyll or Hyde!'

'Hmph. Friends.' Edytha mumbled.

Amiette laughed, sometimes a manic mood had its up-side, and it was impervious to dents at the moment. 'Yes, I'm afraid you're stuck with it now!'

'So, you are Dr Jekyll today?' Edytha narrowed her eyes. 'I will let you know who I prefer.'

Amiette laughed delightedly. Here was a person who spoke her mind, no matter what the social convention.

'If I had to be serious though, I wish you would prefer Mr Hyde – because he's not half so sociable, and might *need* a kick every now and again.'

'I was always very good at kicking.' Edytha admitted with a chuckle. They had been walking aimlessly, or so it seemed, but Edytha pulled Amiette to the side then, saying 'This way!' as she stomped ahead. Leaning up against the wall a little further on was a short tanned man, looking very orange in the filtered light. He had no teeth, and he dragged on a tiquar in such a way that his whole face seemed to be sucked in with it. Amiette didn't trust anything you had to breathe in to your lungs, healthy or not. Edytha approached him almost warily, and spoke in a language Amiette didn't understand. She tapped her 'plant half way through the conversation, and at the end shook his hand in a curious way; elbow to elbow, for which he took off his glove.

Edytha placed something electronic looking into a small pouch and stuffed it into her bag. 'All done! Just an old friend!' She declared, seemingly pleased with herself. 'Where to go now?'

Amiette shook her head in bemusement at all the facets of her new friend, but all in all, she was glad it gave her something else to think of.

10 MISINTERPRETATION

Edytha awoke in her single bed with a patchwork cover. It was actually a present from Oszkár. An unfamiliar lump rose in her throat. Mostly thoughts of Oszkár gave her a spectacular angry haze followed by a headache and very often the only cure was a good sleep. He had found this particular quilt a good decade ago and embedded tracking devices and coded messages into the filaments of the stitching. He wanted her to know that even though they were no longer sharing a bed, he would always know how to find her.

'Stupid old goat!' Edytha declared to no-one in particular. 'Can't find me now can you?' For some reason the anger behind the idea that he would never be able to track her again was sadly lacking. The lump in her throat seemed to grow threefold until it was an unmanageable searing ache.

'Initiate calm protocol. Alpha, lima, delta 449365.' Edytha announced. An internal micro capsule that she had not used since before retirement flooded her bloodstream with Valnor. Her limbs immediately felt a little limp, and her brain was a little fuzzy, but the immediate uncomfortable emotions receded.

'I know, I know! Stupid idea.' She spoke to her husband's twin single bed – stripped and remade, but with linen in his favourite colour – a very deep blue, which she usually took care to leave until last to wash as it didn't match the room. 'Valnor is for raw recruits. But I have a lifetime supply cooped up in there!' She pointed near to her elbow just above a small scar in the cubital fossa.

'Breakfast time Oszkár! Just because you are dead does not mean I can starve myself from pity.'

When the hot water was infusing through a cup of Dark Mint leaves, Edytha opened the pouch she had received from her former colleague yesterday and removed a small update chip. Her heart beat faster despite the Valnor in her system as she placed it on the skin above her implant. She sipped the tea and tried not to wince as the small device burrowed tendrils through her skin to connect and update. Before retirement Oszkár and herself had received regular hard updates. They were considered safer than those obtained from the grid. Not risk free however, as she well knew.

Her screen came to life and scrolled through about fifty images, the final piece of the puzzle.

'Crazy old goat! Irresponsible, ridiculous, good-for-nothing, stupid, crazy old – don't forget the old Oszkár – GOAT! No good comes from coming out of retirement Oszkár. Doesn't matter if you are bored of your life you stupid coot! Or bored of your wife! Hah!' Edytha could feel the lump re-forming. But God in the heavens it was annoying this stupid lump.

'I can't talk to you right now Oszkár. I'm too mad at you. No good ever comes of it.' She rescanned the latest FTT from his unnamed associate looking for clues, dates. Nothing. It was very brief. No VTs either. Probably neither of them knew who the other was. Stupid little hen. Probably gullible. Probably has no idea what he is getting himself into. 'Oskar who have you conned to be your second because this is not government, not forces…' She looked at the coding again. 'Seems pedestrian…but no, too advanced.' She walked round her clean house looking for clues, checked his travel history and came up a blank. She muttered under her breath about new joints and tracking devices.

'Hard to be mad at you right know when you so damn clever you old goat!' She chuckled.

She felt a thrill in her veins. The not quite forgotten adrenaline kick of a puzzle unsolved. 'Initiate caffeine. Alpha, lima, delta 449382.' She looked across at the blue bed. 'Yes, yes I know, but it is your fault after all. If I am to spend all night awake with your crazy games an old brain needs some help, yes?'

*   *   *

Ymarise sauntered up the road to her Tih-Krah session. She needed to enjoy it, take in all the good and release all the bad…Needed this one to last for a while. 'Hey Jule! How are you?' She listened with half an ear to the instructor's small talk wondering why she always had to follow social convention before getting to the point in the conversation where she needed to be. 'Anyway, I'm going to make today my last class for a while.'

'Oh no! That's such a shame! You were doing so well – and you know these manoeuvres should be maintained to keep a healthy life balance!' The green haired instructor had an annoying intonation anyway, Ymarise reasoned she could live without this class.

'Oh not to worry – I'll keep practising at home!' She was not going to start discussing any reasons why, with a woman she hardly knew.

'Well you know what they say – "You are what you practise the most!"' Jule sprang off on tip toes to speak to another group of students. No doubt she practised being a stick thin goddess every day. She probably didn't have children. Ymarise had a stomach that only mothers could be proud of, although the Head of Maths at the University was fond of telling her she was lucky she'd only had one. It always amazed her how mothers of two or three felt they had the right to call her lucky. No amount of sleep loss, heartache or pain could possibly add up to the experience of a mother of two. Never mind the fact that their children played with each other thus lessening the parent's responsibility. She breathed in and slowly out. Take the poisonous thoughts and breathe them out.

She stepped into her place on the third row facing Jule and pushed her toe on to the circle on the floor, activating her zone. She changed the backdrop to jungle and the floor to grass, though in fact it still felt like the spongy rubber she knew it to be.

'Okay ladies let's focus shall we?' Jule reached up to the

ceiling and then folded her elbows down, her fingertips resting on various points on her scalp. 'For those of you who are newer, use your feedback to guide you to the Kah Suh Poh points on the head. Those of you who have been coming a little while should be able to find them easily without guidance – use the spacings we have been through and find the natural undulations in your skull. Now breathe in, and as you breathe out I want you to picture the colour of your body changing to a deep cleansing green, from your fingertips right down to your toes. I'm adding a shade to all your zones, but with time you will feel the cleansing action of these points without the additional stimulus.'

Ymarise loved these sessions. This was her secret single love of technology, probably because her imagination or spirit or whatever it was, never did allow her to feel 'cleansed' when she tried it in her kitchen, complete with Tad scrounging for food or Bracq pottering nearby.

She followed Jule and lifted her face upwards, the zone released warm air and UV synthesised sunlight down on to her face. She walked her feet out towards a Hanoi Hanh pose, sliding her hand down her leg until her finger hit the spot just below the side of her kneecap. Her guidance feedback was switched on in her zone so she felt a warm tingle as her index finger hit the point. She breathed in with the rest of the class and as she breathed out she mirrored Jule to reach just above her ankle to the next point.

When she had first started Tih Krah she had been sceptical, but a lot of the points they used seemed to match the strongest of the old acupuncture points. She had old texts in her department to prove it. Although the Eastern theories had long been disproved, the practise did work, just not in the way they thought it did at the time it was being used. One of these days she should write an article…"Why the craze of Tih Krah is not as original as you thought". It made her smile. She had a great idea for an article most days of the week, but no time to realise all of them. Or perhaps if she was truthful, no inclination. When she was at work she thought she should stay there for ever to get everything she wanted to achieve done, but then as soon as she got home she thought exactly the same about her family life. Neither seemed in balance despite her weekly Tih Krah.

Her zone started changing – all the jungle leaves tinged purple at the tips and an indigo light was descending. Ymarise realised she was behind the rest of the class. She turned to the other side and the light softened back to a pale green.

Bracq sat down heavily on the leather couch. Funny how anything retro reminded him of his wife. He thought of her face: competent, loving, beautiful. He would suffer this indignity to be worthy of his family. So he wiped his slightly sweaty palms on his trousers and looked up to the woman across from him. His eyes flew top left of his screen to check his numbers and then looked back at her. There were five lines of numbers. It helped him calm some of the panic at being stuck on this leather couch. She studied him carefully. 'Tell me about your gambling problem, Bracq.'

Tad practically ran out of school. He scrambled to be first on to the pod and sat in the same seat he always did with the scuff marks on the floor and two diagonal lines broken where a panel of the floor had been put in backwards. His ID tag marked him in to the school pod register. When about eleven other children had got on the pod he breathed on his wrist until the tag got hotter, then took out the cooler section from his lunchbox and placed that against his wrist. He used the next three seconds to scoot through the doorway. Frel and he had watched one of the older boys do this but had never dared try it before. Now his name would be sailing home without him. Frel wasn't on the pod today. He hadn't been partners with him either in Science as he had been told off for talking and moved to sit in front of the teacher.

Frel was going home with Aaron. Aaron's mum was going to pick them up from school: Frel had told him just before lunch. Tad had stayed inside all through lunch – he told Frel he was busy on a drawing.

Tad sat on the wall around the corner from the school pod. He would walk home. Only babies took the pod. He watched Sicily and Gabe walking out – Sicily waved at him and he half waved back, but scooted further round on the wall so no-one could see him as they came out of the gates. A couple of minutes later Aaron and Frel ran out of the blue gates – a very small woman with black hair telling them not to run too far ahead. Frel was wearing an Idaho jacket and so was Aaron. They were like Stones but not as expensive. As they ran the jackets played the pace of their steps across the backs in a sound wave pattern that danced from one jacket to the next. Aaron stopped and slapped Frel on the back. The pattern of his hand rippled outwards to the shoulders making them both laugh.

Tad felt sick. He turned round and got back on the pod. He forgot to trick his ID so his name showed up twice on the list by the window. Maybe the report would be sent to his mum, or maybe they would assume it was a mistake. He didn't care.

Ymarise turned to wave to Jule who was locking the door of the studio. She started to cross the street, checking for cycles and stopped dead. Bracq was three doors down exiting a building she didn't recognise. A woman with dark brown hair had her hand on his shoulder and then waved in a carefree way as he walked away down the street.

The blood inside Ymarise's veins seemed suddenly too loud and too large. She imagined a little green haired angel on her shoulder telling her what to do. 'Calm down, these are poisonous thoughts you are having,' she told herself, 'picture the thoughts as black, infecting your brain, and just breathe them out, one at a time, watch the smoke leave your body.'

She felt stuck between running after him and asking what he was doing in this part of town, and running away to fight the insane thoughts swirling round her head before she spoke to him like a rational adult. 'Don't give in to the negative thoughts!' The green haired waif on her shoulder intoned.

In the end she neither followed him nor ran away, but stepped two steps sideways and fell onto a seat outside a rest-eat. She tapped the table menu and ordered a hot chocolate. Mini-Jule on her shoulder frowned at the choice, as there were green teas and microbial mults on the menu next to it.

When she sipped the chocolate she breathed in slowly. There were a million rational explanations for his appearance here when he had left for his new job this morning. It was not the job of his dreams but it was still a job. He could be buying her a present! No, perhaps not, as their finances were pretty dire right now. There was no way he would be arranging surprises, particularly after they spent so much on Tad's birthday present. He had been very secretive lately about finances, moving credits round and spending more time than usual sitting in his favourite chair and looking over the FTTs from the bank.

She tapped her 'plant and zoomed in on the doorway he had left. There were six nameplates outside. 'Mr J Turnboule, S. Fawsley MD, Lumley & Co, F Shriker, S. Kayne, and G R Tolley.' She searched for the names on the grid with the street name. One was a dental whitening clinic, then a doctor, a holo and massage chair centre and three private addresses.

So he could be seeing a doctor, or getting brighter teeth! No problem! No need for a psychotic break down. She let out the breath she had been holding. A little niggling voice suggested that he would have mentioned seeing a doctor, and wouldn't spend money on his teeth right now. Maybe, just maybe, he'd been playing you for a fool with "S. Kayne". Samantha? Sascha? Maybe the reason why finances continued to be so tight was because he was supporting a secret life she knew nothing about! 'Toxic thoughts!' Screeched the green haired imp. Breathe them out!

Ymarise took in a shaky breath and let it out. How could she breathe out her poisonous thoughts if more kept crowding in to replace them like a sewer?

She dragged her feet to the station practising the smile she would keep fixed to her face when she got home. Breathe. He had been through a tough time and needed the support of his wife now more than ever. Breathe. The last thing he needed was to deal with her insecurities on top of everything else. She imagined the smoky tendrils of noxious thought turning back on themselves and being breathed back in…What if he'd just had enough of scraping by…getting on with it? What if he was just looking for a fresh start? He always said he wished he'd taken more chances. A small part of her brain wondered if he was taking a chance on someone else.

'Ridiculous!' Mini-Jule retorted, her green hair flying. 'Stop feeling sorry for yourself – you're imagining the whole thing! You'll step through the door and he'll tell you all about his free voucher for a white smile and you'll laugh!'

Bracq had done more talking in the last hour than he had probably done in the last six months. What a pious, trumped up, self-congratulating, condescending woman she was! There was not a hope in the universe he was going back to her version of therapy. If he had considered it at all as a younger man he would have assumed you were supposed to feel better after a session not worse! He'd rather quit cold turkey than ever have to go through that again. Besides which, it was hardly a problem. He had stopped off on the way home and not bought a ticket hadn't he – just a six pack of Krug. Before going to see this so-called professional he had been half afraid she might laugh him out of the clinic for having such a small problem it wasn't even worth talking about, and yet inside his pocket he had an unsigned contract which set out his withdrawal from lottery tickets, retinal scrubs, fast threes and any games of chance, and the support he would need to enable him to do that.

What was it about professionals that they just couldn't help but stand on the remnants of your pride and dignity? Yes he enjoyed seeing the numbers in his peripheral vision. Yes it gave him a pleasant escape from his present existence, and yes he felt an urge to replay whenever he won, and he supposed it did stop him sleeping, but for Space's sake, he was having trouble sleeping anyway!

And did he borrow money to gamble – no! Did he skip work to gamble – no! Doctor Kayne had not looked kindly on the fact that he *could* easily have played all day if he wanted to at work…the work he did needed little input from his brain at times…but he chose not to. He did not spend all day wasting credit! And the small amount he did use was nothing compared to the enormity of their current debt. He just needed a bit of help to kick the habit altogether. And now here he was feeling more miserable and more inclined to buy a new line. It was probably what she wanted after all. That was probably her business plan…make all clients feel crappy so they have to keep seeing her for ever. Not this little one. He picked the scrumpled up contract and held it out for the atomic shredder, smiling as it pulverised before his eyes and re-assembled to a freshly pressed sheet.

Ymarise walked through the door. 'Hi!' She smiled widely, 'I thought you didn't like those things since nobody ever uses paper anymore? What was it?'

'Hngh? Oh nothing. I'm going up to get changed.' Bracq grunted.

'Oh, okay.' Ymarise let the smile go as soon as he was out the door.

Bracq caught the tone and sighed. Since when wasn't a grown man allowed to get changed when he wanted? Still, he had to prove to the pompous doctor that his marriage didn't need any more contracts. 'I bought us some food on the way home! Hydrapaks – Tad will love it!'

'Okay, great.' He heard Ymarise shouting back up. Way too many 'okays', and way too much silence. Women! Never happy! She probably wanted something a little more refined, with organic green crap in it. Well tough: if they were cutting back on luxuries her choice of food would have to go. He wasn't going to feel guilty about it. Too many people were trying to load a heap of guilt on to him today.

He walked in to the kitchen and opened the fridge, placing his Krug beers inside. 'Did you tell that woman you were stopping her classes?'

'Yes – all done - all fine!' Oh crap, thought Bracq. If okay was the opposite of okay, then fine was surely anything but fine. He really wasn't in the mood to talk, and suddenly found he had lost the desire to have a nice relaxing drink and a bite to eat. Trust a woman to be so annoying he didn't even feel like eating any more.

'I'm not hungry. I'll keep my Hydra for tomorrow. I'll be upstairs checking my FTTs.'

'Okay! Great!' Ymarise shouted after his retreating back. She would not check his FTTs. She would not. Not. Not. He would just stay upstairs…probably just sit at his desk and roll in to bed at midnight. Not a single thing to worry about. She should probably cook him a snack…or bring him a drink. Nothing out of the ordinary with that…Just a wife doing something nice for her husband.

She heard Bracq before she saw him. He kept his head down, shuffling through some detritus on the kitchen surface, picking at an inconsequential stain on the wall. 'I'm heading out for an hour.'

Crap. Ymarise could barely think over her pounding heart rate, blood seemed to be pumping noisily behind her eyes, in her fingertips. She wouldn't have known without a mirror if she was flushed completely red or drained to near white. She felt as if she had taken a step back from reality.

'Where are you going?' Her best attempt at a normal tone of voice fell sadly flat and almost broke at the end.

'Just out.' Bracq still refused to make eye contact and now sounded angry as well.

Reality became one shade fuzzier as Ymarise fought to control the rising hysteria. 'When do you think you'll be back?' She looked away as her eyes glazed over with tears and lifted her chin up slightly to stop them falling down her cheeks, then blinked rapidly.

Bracq glanced her way thinking how typical it was that he couldn't even have just his own problems to deal with, his bloody family had to get in on the act too. Well, not right now they wouldn't. He was going to have some bloody peace before he had to face the music. 'I'll see you later.' He saw Ymarise lift a hand in farewell and walked out the door hearing it click behind him.

Ymarise felt her stomach drop three inches with the feeling like she'd just downed a shot of Yellow Fire. Surprisingly she didn't cry. She just felt the tears unleash and fall silently down her face. 'Mum!' Tad called from upstairs. Ymarise didn't really recognise she was sobbing until her shoulders were shaking and a strange creening noise emerged unbidden. The more she tried to diminish the noise the louder it got.

'Never mind I've found it!' Tad called down, completely

unaware of the break-down of his peaceful existence. The thought of the possible implications to her son had her crumpling to the floor like a wet sheet of paper. She didn't bother to stop the tears now and then, seemingly from childish contrariness, they abated.

She would have to be strong. What would a strong woman do right now? She had always imagined she was a throwback to the olden days before people became dependent on tech and gadgets. So what would a twentieth century woman do without technology to survive? Find him? Speak to him? She held back the inevitable groan. Speaking to Bracq in his current state of mind was not an option she relished. Nor was finding out which type of woman might have enticed him away from her. She accessed the family network to see where Bracq was located, and oddly enough he had not hidden his whereabouts. His little avatar flashed over the Irish pub 'O'Riley's'. It was in the rougher area between the university and the main shopping mall. The town planners had tried to eradicate the usual associations with industrial warehouses by placing little pockets of businesses and homes between the rows of larger storage areas. It hadn't really worked. The usual associations applied and now included the houses and businesses. Not that Lunar 17 had any serious crime, but you still wouldn't want to walk alone late at night there. She subvocalized a message to her neighbour asking if she could watch Tad for an hour. The answer pinged back almost immediately. Okay, so technology was handy sometimes…

Luckily it was early yet by pub standards, and the pod would get her close by. She used her university pass for a free ride parcwise towards O'Rileys. Bracq had probably walked.

Bracq was sitting nursing a very cool pint. The frost from the cryo bar had even crept up to his knuckles on two fingers which he was sure was against health and safety regs. The guy sitting next to him who looked worse for wear had frosty elbows and slightly frosty hands, but he somehow doubted it was even registering.

Ymarise peered through the window with decorative lead diamond detail. Bracq was wearing his old leather floorduster coat. He looked quietly brooding; slightly menacing even given his current surroundings.

The nerve to approach him had deserted her for the moment. She couldn't quite work out if this was her own anxiety over their argument or whether she was just now remembering how attractive he was. She felt a sudden pang of remembrance as she recalled the moment when they had first hooked up. His jaw and eyebrows had been gripped in a similar frown as he sipped and stared. The world had not been cool enough for him back then: the older brother of a friend, he had reeked of unattainability.

Right now he looked just as untouchable as he had back then. At least there was no female anywhere near. So he was either having an affair but not right at this second, or he was just monumentally pissed at her. Not a great set of options to work with. Ymarise turned round and slunk back home. Her strong and powerful persona would have to come back another day.

About half an hour after she relieved the neighbour she heard Bracq come in and walk straight upstairs to Tad's room.

Tad spoke the moment he walked through the door without pausing to take a breath. 'I've probably got more chance of winning the lottery than ever having my best friend back. Not that I'd want him back. Did you know the chance of winning the interlunar lottery is 13.7 billion to 1?'

'Is it though?' Bracq replied gently.

'Yes and the chances of catching a pod that is the same number as your age on lunar 17 is 247 to 1. So people should just try that instead, because the chances are better and it's exciting when you catch the pod with your age on it isn't it, Dad?'

'My lovely boy,' Bracq whispered, kissing his son on the forehead and brushing back his hair, 'Don't ever change.' He picked up the tablet and put it back to recharge.

'Are you going to make sure Mum's okay?'

Bracq could feel his eyes getting misty, nothing much escaped this child, so he kept his head turned away as he whispered back: 'Good night Tadelesh.'

*   *   *

Dave banged on another random door. Guin watched Therg as he bent next to the door and removed a panel. 'Therg are you doing what I think you are doing?'

'Nothing like being locked in to hasten the activity of what few brain cells exist inside this building.'

'Nothing like willingly locking *ourselves* in to a law

enforcement building' Guin replied as Dave continued up the corridor.

'Relax, Guinevere. It will appear as a malfunction. We could probably complain to them for the considerable trouble it will soon cause us.' As always Therg's expression was indecipherable.

'Alright for you bach, your Dad would have you out before you could say Johnny Jackrabbit!'

'I assure you I would say no such thing. Done. We are sealed inside this building. You may knock on as many doors as you please.'

Dave paused. 'All empty so far. This one looks promising. Look it has a name on it: Moldonny! Just the chap we need.' He raised his hand but grimaced as he saw the receptionist and another officer fiddling with the door. 'Looks like they noticed. I don't think they can be pointing at us, do you Therg?'

'Seems improbable they would want to attract our attention when they explicitly informed us the matter was in hand, and we were to be escorted out of the building.' Therg was not ruffled. 'I say continue knocking. No doubt they will make their sentiments known in due course.'

'Come in!' Fraser called out.

The three students he had seen earlier tumbled into his office and one of them nudged the tall pale one until he spoke.

'Sorry to disturb you. We have some important information that it is imperative you hear.'

'Didn't I send you to talk to Delot?' Fraser cut him off.

'Unfortunately he was unavailable. We have not yet seen anyone beyond the staff at reception, and as I have already explained to her, this is not something I can happily leave as a message for someone else to deal with and leave with a clear conscience. And no, I have no wish to write to Mr Frethun with a full detailed report of my concerns, I very much wish to discuss them today.'

Fraser was impressed, not many younger boys could string together a coherent argument, let alone in a Police Force Building. He wondered about his upbringing, 'What is your surname?'

'Von Thering, sir.'

That would account for it then, Fraser sighed. Boy had probably been brought up debating with his chess coach and his nanny since he was three years old.

'You've got 10 seconds before I discover why you have been left to roam around unescorted.'

Guin explained as Therg had gone silent again. Therg did this at incredibly inconvenient times. Dave chipped in whenever he felt Guin was losing coherency.

Fraser was just about to speak to the front desk when Therg recovered from his latest self-imposed silence.

'The colours match the times.' Therg said calmly.

Fraser's face was a blank. 'Say what?'

The other two looked at the board 'Oh yeah,' Guin replied,

'the wavelength of the colour matches the time – nice find!'

'Russian weirdo!' Dave chipped in, sotto voce, never one to let Therg get big-headed, no matter how astute a brain he had.

Fraser frowned, 'Hold on, back up! There's a link between these events?'

Therg ignored him, seemingly bored already. Dave explained patiently how the colours of the jewels matched the times of the theft. 'See this, here, it's a ruby, so it's red, right? The wavelength of the colour red is six hundred and fifty…6:50…get it? Orange is 600, green is 520.'

Guin interrupted… 'Hold up gents' – he rubbed his hands together – 'I know that expression! Something big Therg? Go on my son! Get in there!'

'It's like a puzzle!' Announced Therg, 'Ingenious!' He paused and smiled a rare smile. 'Got it.'

'Yesss! Get in!' Guin pumped the air with his hand, making up for Therg's apparent lack of celebration.

Fraser pulled his lips closed, trying not to drag the reluctant words from this big lump of a boy with the solemn face.

Dave smiled, 'Put him out of his misery, mate – this board deserves an answer!'

They all look at the underlined, circled, and re-underlined scribbles on the board. '3am job was it?' laughed Guin.

Well? Fraser finally found he could stifle his interest no longer. 'What's the other big thing?'

'You won't believe it.' Therg rubbed his chin contemplatively. 'I barely believe it... But I checked. Twice.' He paused again, and Fraser nearly did a little dance of frustration on the spot. 'The sunshine yellow, as you point out here, is actually an orange diamond. Diamond is formed by carbon, number 6 on the periodic table, and the orange part from a nitrogen impurity, seventh on the periodic table, giving a total of 13, or 1, 3, or indeed, if you prefer, 1st of the 3rd. Now, here's where it gets tricky... The part of ruby that gives it its colour is an oxide of chromium, atomic weight 24, or if you prefer, the 2nd of the 4th month. Emerald gets its green from either chromium or vanadium, or both, and if we assume both, that gives you a combined atomic weight of 47 – you guessed it – 4th of July. Now Guin Fenwick –you may tell me I am brilliant.'

'A-bloody-crappin-mazing, bach!' Guin reached up for a high five but Therg merely looked at the hand in puzzlement.

'No?' Guin exclaimed in annoyance. 'Leave me hanging would you? You are not playing yourself in our film either! Talking about our film...does this mean he's going to deal with our problem now?'

Fraser finally found his voice 'Are you joking?' His mind was racing. Who was this thief? Why did it not seem to fit with the image he had of Tuula? Who in their right mind thinks up such grand strategies for robberies?

'Nope' Dave piped up, 'I just checked it – he's right - I never would have got it though – it takes a fine knowledge of jewellery and chemistry that I quite frankly do not have any desire to possess.'

Okay – I will personally see the manager of the Museum about your coronal ...thing, if you tell me one more thing: What time and day would a sapphire give us?'

There was a unanimous silence for a couple of seconds – Therg answered just before Dave. '5am, 4th of the 8th.'

Guin accessed his plant and muttered about Titanium and iron, his eyebrows dancing in concentration, before concurring. 'That's tomorrow morning, just after our flare, in fact.' he added.

'Of course it is.' Fraser took a deep breath. He subvocalized commands for searches on the grid. This time cross referencing his top list of blue gems with the new date. He skim-read the info with a sinking feeling: Lunar 17, Guillaume Memorial Museum, Stem Cell Research August Charity Ball & Auction, 4th August. 3rd largest sapphire in existence on loan from private owner Selène Langevin for this event only. He hardly dared, as his gut knew what was coming but he brought up the guest list never the less...Shit.

11 ANGER

Fraser ran full pelt down the corridor and almost smacked into a door that was usually open, with several people on the other side speaking to holos and gesticulating wildly at the door.

'Ahh, common problem inside governmental buildings this, let me see if I can help. Announced Therg, who seemed to have glided along behind him.

The door slid open after very little trouble.

Fraser narrowed his eyes. 'You're very lucky I have important things to do right now.' He made the gesture from both his eyes to all three boys. 'Don't go anywhere.'

'Jourdaine!' He shouted. 'I need these three kept here. They may be vital to my current investigation.'

Guin began to protest. 'And give them food!' Fraser

added, 'Whatever they want!'

'Thanks butt!' Guin grinned, 'Crisis averted!'

Fraser could just about hear the pale one telling the welsh one that his stomach was a crisis it was impossible to avert. He jogged out of the door and tapped his 'plant. 'Tuula!'

Tuula came on line immediately, 'Jeez you scared me! What is it? I'm at work!'

'I need you to go somewhere private. Right now!'

Tuula looked around her at the water plant, her heart thumping painfully. 'I literally can't see another soul. What is it? Are you in trouble?'

'I need to be really honest...No this isn't going to work. I need to see you, face to face. Can you meet me? Like right now?'

Tuula tapped her plant and raced to the side of the building towards the patch of rough ground between their border and the number nines, hoping she would be lucky and catch a pod quickly. It involved straddling a fence that had been beaten to almost ankle height by the volume of illicit pedestrian traffic, as most staff who worked on this side of the plant found it quicker to catch a nine and then a 1 than walk to the front for a 2.

Oh God, she thought, this was probably it, he was finally going to dump her. Why else would he need to see her than to deliver bad news? She willed herself in to a walk. Why was she hastening towards that evil fate? Did she want to be dumped with sweat marks? Or was he actually working some horrible case and his life was at risk? Was hers at risk? She glanced round. There was nobody at the pod stop. She looked over the edge at the water slopping on to the concrete. Not a common time of day to catch a pod; it was literally deserted. Was that a bad thing? Was she in more danger? She took a deep breath – this was ridiculous…she was in all likelihood about to be dumped. At least if she could be dumped her worries about her relationship status were ungrounded…you didn't have to dump a woman you only associated with for a big case.

She tapped her plant again and spoke to a holo of Fraser. 'I'm walking towards you right now along the wharf path. If I see a pod I'll catch it.'

'Great. I'm walking 1 rimward towards you.'

'What's going on?'

'I thought we were doing this face to face?' Fraser reasoned.

'I can see your face its right there!' Tuula reached in front of her and slashed through his holo face, wobbling the pixels in finger shaped swathes.

'Ha ha. I want to speak to you privately.' Fraser was not going to have this conversation where it could be monitored and he wasn't sure who he was protecting most: her or him.

'Hang on I see a pod.' Tuula ran the last 10 metres and jumped from the wharf to the pod just as the doors slid closed. She scanned her wrist for the fee.

'Well that was interesting!' Fraser grinned at her.

Tuula groaned – seeing someone run on a holo image was not at all flattering and she normally swapped to voice only when doing anything that did not involve a normal and still face forward conversation. She could even admit to herself that she had set up her holo to show her from left 29 degrees as this was her favourite angle of her own face. Pathetic to have wasted time on that. The exact kind of pathetic girl with nothing better to do who was about to be dumped by her exciting boyfriend. 'Can we please just pretend you can wipe the last thirty seconds from your memory?'

'You can pretend all you like.' Fraser laughed. 'My retina just burned the image straight into long-term memory! Hey I think you're coming to where I am.'

'Yes I see you – hang on I'm just getting off.' There were no crowds at this time of day so no exaggerated 'exit' movements to make for the benefit of those pressed in next to you, and no sweaty bodies to squeeze past to get to the door. It was actually heavenly to glide out and feel a light breeze. Fraser picked her up at the waist and span her round. As usual her heart stuttered in his presence. The strong arms, the clean smell of him, the light dancing in his eyes as if they were always sharing a joke just with her, all melded together to create a blow to her senses every time. She took comfort in the fact that these were not the actions of a man desperate to be free. Or at least, not in her experience.

'Let's walk.' Fraser tugged her along with an arm around her slight shoulders and felt her shiver. 'Cold?'

'No I'm fine – not with your great big self blocking me from the wind!' Tuula smiled.

'Less of the big, you. Here, look, we can sit here.' Fraser checked the area for surveillance but he knew from experience it was a dead zone as it frustrated his colleagues from time to time.

Tuula stared at the spire of a GGP building, trying not to hurry the words that Fraser was seeming to find difficult to spit out. At last she sighed and gave up. 'So you said something about being honest?'

'Listen,' Fraser started and paused again, 'this party you are going to at the Memorial Museum. Do you absolutely have to go? No…What I mean is, if I asked you not to go would you listen?'

'That is not what I was expecting you to say. Did I really just leave my job to meet you for an emergency discussion for you to ask me not to go to some random ball?'

'Some random ball!' Fraser repeated, 'Only you could –' He stopped when he saw her expression. 'Okay, okay, I'm sorry!' He scrunched up his face and sighed.

'And yet you still aren't telling me what's going on.' Tuula pursed her lips.

'There might be trouble there tonight.'

'My parents will be there! What kind of trouble?' Tuula whispered.

'Can you not just trust me this once and not go?' Fraser was looking exasperated.

'I obviously can't just stay behind and leave all my friends and family to go in blind to whatever scenario scared you enough that I shouldn't –' She stopped talking when she saw Fraser looking exasperated...or maybe even...slightly embarrassed? 'Unless...am *I* the trouble?'

Fraser winced. He was not handling this conversation at all well. How did she see the finer nuances as she did? What kind of intelligence could read a situation so accurately? A little voice told him what he least wanted to hear. Maybe she was just too close to him. Maybe she was throwing him off his game.

'Am I a suspect in this trouble Fraser?? Is this what you are *not* telling me so well?'

'Yes!' Fraser blurted out. 'Jesus that hasn't changed! If you are so innocent just don't go! There'll be a whole SWAT team waiting to take you out!'

'I guess if you trusted me, or thought anything of my integrity you wouldn't be here right now would you? Why should I have to prove myself to you?'

'Are you asking me to love you no matter what?' Fraser shouted, 'Because you surely must know that my career kinda negates the need for me to answer!'

'I think I need to think about this.' Tuula said woodenly, standing up. 'I think I need to think long and hard about who needs me here, given my family could be walking in to an international patch of "trouble".' She started to walk away and then turned back to find Fraser staring at her still. 'And maybe I should think about how I've been a suspect to you all along. You're right. Nothing has changed.'

'Tuula!' Fraser shouted, but she walked faster in the opposite direction. He scuffed his boot against the loose chalk and swore. He actually didn't have time for this. Instinct told him that this was a hurt girl and not a con. But either way, he had things to do.

*   *   *

Tad picked the pink tissue out of his jumper as he turned right out of the school gates. He found himself in a slow moving trail of kids heading to the wharf. He was actually surprised they had gone to so much trouble. None of the toilets at school stocked pink toilet paper.

Most of the boys had all run ahead and were even now catching the pod that had just arrived. A couple of girls from behind him sprinted ahead to catch it. Tad scuffed his shoes noisily. He didn't want to catch that one anyway. He preferred to be alone. Having friends was pointless.

He sat on the edge of the wharf with his shoes dangling in to the water soaking up the wet. He didn't care. Probably would be cool to get caught by the pod driver with his feet dangling right next to the sign which warned against such behaviour. As it happened the driver didn't see or didn't care and Tad swung his feet out of the way just as it approached. He sat slumped on the bristly seat and put his wet feet up on the seat next to him, effectively blocking anyone from attempting to be friendly. He was pleased to see that he had left a muddy stain on the blue of the seat. He wondered what the punishment would be for staining public property. Maybe his Dad would get another FTT. Didn't matter anyway. He watched his stop go past with a blank expression on his face. The route was familiar as it took him straight to the Parc and he had visited his Dad there plenty. Feeling an odd need to burst out of his comfortable routine he gazed around the busy station and chose a random pod rimwise. Number 7. It had purple seats instead of blue. This gave him a vague sense of satisfaction so he sat back and watched the high rise flats drift past.

When he saw a patch of gold on top of one of the buildings he got off, reminded of the golden hand that had saved his namesake. But when he peered at it after the pod had disappeared it was just the letters of the corporation who owned the building HBOS. Still, it felt right to follow his destiny so he idled along the path. He turned left when he saw a golden wrapper lying twisted on the floor and right when the brass coloured window fixings caught the sun.

His legs felt tired. He was ravenously hungry. It was precisely the time he usually started to listen out for his mum getting home. He wondered if she would be surprised he wasn't there. Would she notice or would she be crying again? Would Mrs Mackleby from next door come over again and bring her stupid prickly pear cactus for him to be interested in? There was *nothing* Mrs Mackleby could tell him about *anything*. She didn't even know its scientific name!

It was getting dark. Dark in the sense that the artificial illumination was on its running down programme. Tad never usually found this disturbing as he didn't particularly like the fake daylight anyway. But he did start to wonder why his greater galactic plan might send him to a street at dusk with no shops, no lights and no people. He carried on walking.

Approximately 97 million kilometres away the magnetically drenched solar plasma of an unprecedented coronal mass ejection was still releasing energy at a phenomenal rate. The bright leading edge had left a typically less active sun spot ten hours ago and was still spearing outwards at over 3000 kilometres a second.

Tad felt the knawing of hunger in his stomach; he imagined the acid inside writhing around looking for fresh prey.

He had begun to see people again. He had walked to an area he had never seen before, but at least there were adults around. Some of them had shiny clothes and dresses on though and a few were giving him odd glances. He turned into a well-lit foyer as if he knew where he was going. He had learnt that this was a useful trick to use on adults. A bright smile and a determined stride would get him inside most places that looked interesting and he harboured a desire to see. He climbed three staircases and wandered down a few corridors. Some were cordoned off and he caught glimpses of dark exhibit cases. The shinily-dressed people seemed to all be heading for the same place. He circled the entrance a few times but found little to interest him in amongst the noisy adults. He descended a level and shucked his bag off his shoulders and sat on it. His back rested up against the pedestal of something or other. It looked arty and didn't grab his notice. The beetle that ran over his fingers was a much better prospect to study. He wondered if Frel might like to see it, but then he remembered he didn't have a jar. And then remembered he hadn't spoken to Frel in a week. He squashed the beetle in one swift thump of his hand. As he picked the crushed wings and bloody spatter off his skin the tears rolled down his cheeks.

Tad startled to hear voices coming closer. What his dad called the aristocracy. He didn't really know what that meant but he remembered the tone and sounds of the words they used, even the spacing. He flung his bag over one shoulder and ran. When his heart was pounding and he had no idea where he was, he stopped running. There was a door marked with a no entry sign which pushed open and he found himself outside again. A rain pattern had started and was gloriously consistent: he was soaking wet in about thirty seconds. A corner of his brain thought this was probably for the best as adults tended to notice unaccompanied children, especially those with tears on their faces. They wouldn't see his now. He could still feel the salty water mingling with the fresh, but they would never know.

He sat down on the edge of a vent looking out at the city beyond. He couldn't see anything familiar at all. 'Where's my GGP, mum?' He whispered into the rain. He didn't feel the tiniest bit lucky right now.

12 LOVE

Tuula turned the music up in her flat past the point where the automatic warning intoned the standard safety notice.

'You will damage your eardrums.' Jaimie said cheerfully. 'And mine come to think of it.'

'Go away!' Tuula ran past him.

'I love you too.' Jaimie replied easily. She had long since taught him that sometimes when she needed space she would tell him to go away but it didn't mean she had stopped loving him. The idea had stuck.

Tuula snapped back around and shouted to her brother, 'What are you doing?'

Jaimie was heading out the door as he shouted back 'Erm…Therapy is cancelled so I'm going out!'

Tuula knew Jaimie didn't lie easily and he would often tell her what he wasn't doing rather than misrepresent the truth. 'What's in the backpack?' She tried another tack.

'Climbing stuff.'

'I thought you hated climbing now?'

Jaimie didn't answer. Not that this was unusual. If the question didn't interest him he often did not deign to answer it. Tuula tried one last time just to make sure he would be out of harm's way tonight, 'You're not going to that charity thing with mum and dad tonight are you?'

'I wasn't invited.' Came the swift reply. The door closed behind him.

Tuula tried not to think about Fraser as she raced around her room choosing and disregarding seven dresses before finally picking up the red shorter layered cocktail dress that she had tried on first.

Fraser snapped the buckle on his utility belt into place for the fifth time in the last ten minutes. Varn looked over and rolled his eyes. 'Did you brief the B section?' Fraser asked before he could comment.

'They are waiting for your command.' He tossed his head towards the concealed unit. 'What is it in that head of yours, hmm? Is your princesse inside?'

Fraser sighed. 'In all probability, I would say yes.'

'And you did not warn her away because you believe she is

guilty?'

Fraser grimaced. 'If she *is* guilty then I'm a chinaman. No, I did warn her. I think she'll come anyway.'

'Ahh.' Varn tapped the side of his nose with a smug knowing look, 'The famous Moldonny finesse has wooed your lady friend to trembling obedience again I see.'

Fraser frowned. 'She thinks I should love her on a whim! No questions asked!'

Varn jerked his head to stare at Fraser in surprise 'She asked you to love her? Vraiment?'

'No, no! I think I said it… No, I think I said I couldn't love her no matter what! I have a career! I have –' Fraser stopped talking in the face of Varn's continuous scorn.

'My friend…The first time you mention love to a woman…Oh no no.' He continued to shake his head as if no words could truly represent what a complete balls-up Fraser had made.

'Crap.' Fraser whispered. He rubbed his hand over his face. 'What time is it?'

Varn checked his watch. 'You have six minutes.' He whispered back. 'I will be covering for you from here.' Varn watched Fraser lop off, and still shook his head, wearing the same mildly bemused expression on his face.

Fraser entered a side door and took the back stairs. He passed one startled waiter only. In black combat gear he was not exactly dressed to blend in.

He stayed on the edge of the crowds ducking behind pillars and weaving around display cabinets. As luck would have it he saw Tuula skipping out the far door. He would have recognised her anywhere: the pale ankles, the neat swing to her hips as she walked. But tonight his robin was even wearing red. It almost made him chuckle.

He took a slight detour to get out the way she had gone without being seen, and guessed the route she must have taken by the slight breeze coming from an open door further down.

'Tuula!' He spoke to her softly but she didn't turn. Her gaze was fixed, riveted in shock, on a little boy standing right on the edge of the roof.

*   *   *

Edytha had not visited the grave for a week, it was the longest she had gone yet, and she felt at once liberated and sad, that such a situation had come to pass. The bleep in her ear warned her that a new FTT had arrived, and she gave up eating lunch in the hope of more interesting events. Fate did not disappoint.

The FTT had a highly ornate yet formal header, and was crowded with the formal language of the law. After ten minutes and several sentence re-reads, Edytha deduced that her husband's lawyer had some object or document for her. An unfamiliar address was given. Edytha was not aware they had any other lawyers than those used by the government during the time of their career for wills, identities, and any other legal documents that needed to be procured or forged.

During the pod ride to the padding station she counted the number of women that seemed likely to be influenced by hypnotic suggestion, standing in the queue to the Earth pad she analysed all the body language and facial expressions, and tried to decide who was most likely to be having an affair. Two definites. Three maybes.

The address was in Burbank, within the Hollywood Dome, for which Edytha was grateful. She did not relish going to any areas that were not invitation only, which made her wonder which favours her husband had called in to get there in the first place.

The building had over a hundred different businesses within it. She took the fast elevator to the 14th floor. Saunders & Saunders, in contrast to its name, appeared to be a one man show. It occupied one room, which was a little dreary and old fashioned. Edytha would have thrown open the window for a week, and torn down the blinds if she had owned it.

She was ushered into a battered chair, which was stuck at one height, and vibrated a little. The man was on the short side, but with even, friendly features. His introduction was unassuming; he was a little boring, but pleasant.

'I inherited this business from my father,' he began to explain. 'The item I have for you was left during his "reign", as it were.' He smiled at his own wit. 'I'll get it now.'

He rummaged in his desk and brought out a small but bulging envelope that was slightly faded, and a newer, slimmer, whiter one.

'You would have had these sooner, except we didn't learn

of your husband's death until last week. I do apologise for the delay.'

Edytha took them and quickly submerged them in her handbag. She had intended to find a nice spot to read them, but in the end, curiosity overtook her in the foyer of the building.

She peeled open the envelope and wondered why he had not made a digital missive. She sighed, he had been superstitious even then. The letter was in Russian, it began: *We do not talk our own language enough my dearest one, so I have decided to write this last to you, in our own tongue. Yesterday (I should perhaps mention the year is 2412, you may remember the little job we just finished at this time) I prayed that I would not outlive you, and then I wondered if that was selfish, for then you would be the one to suffer after I had gone. Today I am praying we go together in a spectacular fashion, and that neither of us gets to sit in this dingy office reading notes.*

Edytha smiled, it was odd that you could still have the same thoughts as your husband even after death.
She continued reading: *My beautiful Edytha, light of my life. It is not often that you will hear me be so poetic, but thinking of death makes me unusually eloquent. I realised today when the mission took a difficult turn –*

'Hah! Difficult turn' was a mild way to put it, but Oszkár had always amused their colleagues with his Russian stoicism back in the day. Edytha realised her cheeks were wet, and continued the letter:

-that all my life has been dedicated to protecting you. I really hope, my loveliest wife, that my actions speak louder than the words I will very rarely say. If I ever fail you by quitting this world before you, it gives me just a little happiness to know that for once in your life you will not

doubt the entirety of my feelings for you: I love you with all my heart, my stubborn, wilful and supremely skilful wife. This life we have chosen inspires me to great heights. But I wonder if you ever guessed the true reason for my inspiration? You like to call me your outrageous adrenaline seeker…and who knows what other names you have managed to come up with since I wrote this, my darling? However, the truth is less than heroic, for my main reason for doing this job is that I can spend all day with you, and know that I have done everything in my power to keep you from harm.

Edytha felt the heat in her eyes, coupled with a painful pressure somewhere between her throat and her chest. The pressure to release yet more tears was mounting, and there, in the foyer of a Burbank high rise she sobbed, crying for the love she had lost, the arguments she had started and the time she had wasted. She was quite happy that no-one disturbed her peace…bloody human beings too scared to say the wrong thing would rather ignore a sobbing woman than approach her. Except Amiette – she could be quite impenetrably happy… or maybe not, depending on which way her crazy brain was leaning.

She dried her eyes using a linen handkerchief Oszkár had given her. It had an emergency beacon sewn in to the hem. She smiled another watery smile. Stupid old lovable goat.

It took her 24 minutes to walk to the padding station and almost double that to queue for the return trip. She spent the first two minutes worrying. Worrying was quickly discarded as a fruitless emotion used by the weak of mind. Edytha's mind was not weak. She opened the summary document she had been keeping of everything she knew about Oszkár's dead-in-the-water little hen. He was a boy, and from various references he had let slip she guessed him to be between the ages of 20 and 25. It seemed he had skills in coding, maths, physics, planning. Oszkár had seemed content to let him work out the kinks and keep him supplied with high spec equipment. She had no idea of his name beyond the J he signed off with. She knew from what she had decoded there was a small heist planned for tonight. Oszkár had promised to listen in on police channels remotely to ensure a clean event.

As Edytha stepped off the padding deck back on Diakon she felt the sizzle through her veins. 'Not even time to get home and have a nice tea before you put me to your dirty work Oszkár!' She muttered, settling herself on the bench near his grave.

Hopping her signal over three lesser known stations (just to be sure) she accessed the secure lines used by the LPD Police Force. 'Oh my little hen!' She exclaimed to herself under her breath. 'You are indeed swimming into troubled waters.'

She tripled the encryption she normally used and replied to the FTT that had been sent to Oz. She had no notion whether it would be read in time, but she felt hope, and a small amount of compassion for a complete stranger. It read: "Apologies for information delay. This is Oszkár's oldest and most trusted partner. Please abort. Evidence points towards LPDPF sting. Over and out."

It seemed surreal to her to be signing off for the final time for her husband. Surreal but oddly satisfying that it should be her to complete his final mission. She was a little disappointed she hadn't found his code to be able to subvocalise or holo direct. She stopped dead and cackled to herself. 'Initiate protocol SPIDER V8. Send to LPDF17 secure line AP7982.' She smiled to herself imagining the complete lack of coordination and communication that would ensue in their little sting. If that didn't give Oszkár's little hen a fair river of escape she didn't know what would!

She smiled as she walked aimlessly, admiring the dusty pathway in the orange glow, for once happy to be hobbling slowly and taking in the view. She let her mind wander a little, back over missions, allowing herself to smile at the still slightly raw reminiscences, but without lingering too long on any one memory. Just riffling through them and dipping in here and there without gouging up too much emotion. She noticed her surroundings again as she approached the hydropod station in town. A young woman was walking towards her: unmarried, fashionable, high disposable income, threat - negligible. 'Damn crazy conditioning' Edytha muttered to herself as she searched for a suitable vendor of coffee.

*   *   *

Fraser felt his adrenaline kick-start his brain to a new gear. 'Hi,' He said gently, standing still, 'I'm Fraser.'

Tad stared at the small lady in the red dress with the crinkly edges, and the man all in black with the nice face. The tears had long since dried in tracks down his face, and the rain programme had finished as abruptly as it started.

'I didn't...I mean I wasn't, going to...you know.' Tad told the man. 'I just needed some space.'

'I can understand that.' Fraser smiled. 'Why don't I help you down?'

Tad sniffed and nodded. The next few seconds would occur in a blur but would never be forgotten. Fraser would later report that there were so many things happening at once that it was very difficult to place them in an exact chronological order.

The alarm was tripped in the museum and several guests shouted out in panic. A slight figure of a boy with brown hair blowing in the wind abseiled down a buttress not 4 metres from where they were standing. Tuula gasped and stared in horror at the retreating figure. The noise of the alarm, coupled with the sudden movement downwards of the abseiling figure to Tad's left, through him a little off balance. His eyes widened and his arms started to windmill in thin air. Fraser saw Tad pass the point of no return and started to sprint towards the edge of the roof. As his foot gained the edge, he spun his BunG grapple-hook behind him. Tuula watched in frozen horror as both went over the edge.

Fraser felt a second of sickening free fall before he grabbed Tad's ankle and felt the line pull taut almost in unison. The retraction catapulted them back up and down several times before the stretch came under control. Tad scrambled up the rope like a little monkey despite Tuula's anxious entreaties from above. Fraser reappeared slightly less elegantly and considerably more out of breath. Fraser swore when he tried to get hold of Varn and came up with static on all comms, as he watched the figure with a large back pack run off into the distance below.

'What's your name kid? Are you okay?' Fraser asked, still trying to regain his breath. Tad mumbled his name and nodded but clutched his freshly healed ankle, it rested at a strange angle yet again. 'It's okay...' He winked at the boy. 'It might hurt like hell now but we'll use Police contacts - get you the fastest painkillers and the coolest brace you've ever seen!'

Tuula hovered, like a shy cat about to scramble to safety. 'Will you two be okay? I've got to go.' Tuula looked from Fraser to Tad, and back again. 'There's something I need to do.'

'Who was it?' Fraser demanded, eyes narrowed.

Her eyes were dark in her very pale face, and her bottom lip trembled but she didn't speak as she turned and fled.

The cloud of protons and electrons crossed the final few seconds to the shimmering layer separating Lunar Protectorate Dome 17 from the ravages of space. Five cells were damaged in the ensuing solar storm. Spectators below thought it was an exciting part of the festivities at first. The Cryo-Reseal and Automatic Repair process dealt with all five cells. Although no atmosphere was lost, and the thick glass shield unit beneath was left intact, the ionospheric disturbance caused a temporary change in one of the main exhibits in the Guillaume Memorial Museum.

Fraser spoke to Tad quickly, hoping to deposit him somewhere quickly. 'Are your parents near here?'

Tad didn't reply but Fraser followed his line of sight to a flickering of the light surrounding the metal sculpture 'The Impossible'. It was aptly named, as the entire structure was suspended by magnetism (or at least, he seemed to remember it being described that way for the press release) and the lowest, and extremely sharp, point was a mere 1.8 metres off the ground, leaving tourists the dubious pleasure of walking directly beneath it. A creaking groan filled the air around them and a large whoosh of air followed as the entire assembly fell with a deafening crash.

As Fraser looked over the edge he could see part of the foyer showed jagged edges as The Impossible had ploughed easily through the roof and walls of the museum and pulled them down with it. The top of the sculpture was near to where he had last seen the loan figure with the backpack scamper off. He was torn between hoping Varn had set up a perimeter, hoping there was no slight figure squashed beneath, and hoping the slight figure had made a clean exit.

He saw Tuula slip through a side door below and run full sprint towards the tip of the statue. I guess they'd all know if the squashed boy theory was true in about five minutes. She knew that boy. And if the speed of her sprint was anything to go by she cared about that boy. It had been too small for the Dad, and the only other person in this society he knew she would protect was…

Tad's eyes were still wide open. He had barely sat down from being hauled back from the brink of death when the explosion of sound had sent his heart rocketing again. He tip toed to just behind the detective and peered over the edge. The funny metal twisted shape had settled into its own imprint but the dust was still settling from the stuff it had messed up on its way down. Tad saw a glint of gold and refocused his gaze to the lawman's shoulder. Five golden strips. When he scrunched his eyes up he could almost imagine they were a golden hand.

He smiled at Fraser and replied as if a giant sculpture fell down every other day. 'Mum and Dad aren't here. They are probably looking for me right now though. I probably shouldn't be out this late…or here…at all.'

Fraser attempted to subvocalise to Varn and this time it

went through. *'VARN, HAVE A SITUATION HERE. BOY FOUND NEAR EDGE OF ROOF POSSIBLE JUMPER. NEED TRANTIS OR CHLOELLE UP HERE. WHERE ARE YOU? DID YOU SEE THE BGW JUST BEFORE THE IMPOSSIBLE CAME DOWN?'*

As he sent that message he saw a stream of other messages scroll past mainly on the lines of 'What the hell's going on?' And then an official summary of the magnetic disruption event.

Varn's reply was typical: *'SO WHICH CAN WE ELIMINATE THE B G OR W?'*

'I'LL FILL YOU IN LATER ABOUT THE BOY/GIRL/WHATEVER. WHERE'S TRANTIS?'

'BE CALM MY FRIEND, I SENT HER TO YOUR LOCATION ALREADY.'

To Tad he said 'Can you contact them?'

'I'm inhibited for sends, only family receives.' Tad replied solemnly.

'Here let me give you an override.'

Trantis appeared just as he reconfigured the plant. 'Oh and one more thing…' He sent a message to Tad with a code to pass on to the medical centre. 'Get that ankle seen to!'

13 FULFILMENT

Amiette sat slumped on the seats facing the Texor pad entrance. She had been sitting there for an undeterminable amount of time. The vast emptiness of her day spread ahead of her. Genilh had left her life yet again through that door. And her life now seemed colourless without him near. Was this how her life would be from now on? Cut in to clear segments of colour and darkness? Would she be a constant waiting shadow, devoid of any purpose until her only son came back to visit?

She forced herself to start walking. Determined not to be that shadow. Time to take the meds. Time to keep a diary. Time to stay active.

As she meandered she watched a young mum screeching at her toddler and dragging him in a shoulder dislocation special manoeuvre that only mums get away with. She watched a shuffling man pick at his threadbare cuffs with total absorption. She watched as a slightly dumpy woman with bowed legs but a determined stride make a beeline for her.

'Amiette. I cannot find a single place to drink tea! You must come with me. By the time I find somewhere for tea I will no doubt need coffee. And by the time coffee actually arrives in this Godforsaken town I will need food. We must eat –' she stopped to consult her watch 'Hmmm, Sunday supper.'

Amiette could feel the polite affirmative being uttered almost without recourse to her brain. Edytha had a firm hold of her elbow and was steering her with a surprisingly steely grip. She was talking in a steady stream. Amiette had felt dead inside for so many hours she felt as if her own minimal responses could have come out of someone else's mouth. Her insides felt sluggish.

The talking had stopped. Her strange Russian friend was looking at her expectantly. What had she just said? Some comment about Mr Hyde? Something about a goat?

'Bah never mind!' Edytha continued. I think I prefer this Dr Jekyll anyway. She talks less and doesn't argue with me. And she doesn't prance ahead and get in my way when we are supposed to be walking in straight line.

Amiette felt a flicker of hope that in finding someone who embraced her darker side, there might be some meaning to her existence in the washed out segments of her life. Perhaps all she needed was a very strange friend.

Edytha was staring at a menu and muttering about prices.

'Are we going in here?' Amiette asked.

'Ha! Padlo! She deigns to speak! Good morning pudding head! Yes we will go in here. Choose first though. I need to fix the prices. These ones are no good. No good at all.'

Amiette was well aware that in certain situations when in Edytha's company it was best to have a deaf ear. She took comfort in the fact that sometimes she 'fixed' the prices up as well as down. All was according to Edytha's own notion of fair and right, and often involved much huffing and consigning of various things and people to Hell.

'I'll have the Full Glazed Pot...and I am not a pudding head!'

'Da, yes, not *now* with the pudding head. Your eyes can't see through all the pudding in head ten minutes ago.'

'Edytha I swear your accent gets thicker the longer I've known you! Can we go in yet?'

Edytha chuckled and spoke an unintelligible string of sounds 'Prijateljstvo se ne bira, rekao je, ono biva, ko zna zbog čega, kao ljubav'. As they sat in the corner booth made of real not synthetic wood, she huffed her way through sitting and then explained: 'No-one knows why we find friends – it just happens, like love. But can only be your true self with true friend. Oskar and I would shout happily at each other with accent heavy as a dog, but save perfect English accent for work.'

'Which reminds me! Alibi for my little Hen.' She froze in concentration as she subvocalized and read various items on her screen. She clicked her tongue against her cheek. 'That should do it. Where were we?'

Amiette smiled. Definitely a deaf ear required.

* * *

Fraser lifted a hand up to Varn in greeting as he jogged up to the huddle of Lawmen and spoke to him in a whisper. 'I've swept the whole area and I can't see her!'

Varn put a hand on his shoulder. 'The sapphire has gone. They also scanned the area: there are no bodies under this…thing here.' He gestured lazily to the sculpture. 'Can you place her when the alarm went off?'

Fraser pulled Varn around away from the others even further. 'Placing her is not my problem…But I have a feeling placing her brother might turn out to be an issue.'

'Ah, so you think…the underestimated brother? It is possible.' Varn paused and scratched the back of his head, summing up Fraser's life in a single frowning scrutiny. 'It might well be… how shall I say?…better this way… if we…did not have this conversation, my good friend.'

Fraser sighed. 'You could be right. I think I just need to see how it plays out. Thanks Varn: you're too good to me.'

Varn smiled. 'Bah.'

Fraser figured this was as good as he would get.

Varn nudged him and flicked his eyes towards the boy wrapped in a blanket, still sitting with Trantis. A tall woman and man were running towards him. As they got closer Tad stood up hesitantly and the blanket fell to the floor. The mum got there first and wrapped him in a hug so tight the poor kid was probably choking. She promptly burst in to tears. The Dad put his arms round both of them. He looked tired. It was always oddly reassuring to reunite lost children with their parents. Even in the middle of a crisis. Even with a home burnt to cinders around them there was always that tangible sense of pure love that can create a home inside one hug.

Fraser needed to make that connection and he couldn't bloody find her.

Jaimey sat down heavily on a bench next to a couple and their son. He had watched the kid talking to his parents from where he was hiding in a shrub behind the bench, he had cried for a bit, been hugged, and finally had fallen asleep all wrapped up in a blanket with his head on his Dad's lap and his feet on his mum's. He had heard them talking about something called a GGP. The kid had said "I believe now Dad" some time before he'd zonked out. What interested him more was what the man was saying to the woman afterwards. He didn't hear it all but there was something about a lost job, a pile of debt, some other problem that made the woman cry so he couldn't hear what was said.

He had made the steal on the dot at the correct time and the correct day. That was really all that mattered. Oz was out of the picture. Some friend of his had helped a bit at the end, but really all the hard work was to get the time right. Now he wasn't really bothered too much with the rest of it. His project was finished. Who needed therapy anyway? He was glad his Dad was rich and he didn't have a pile of debts. He didn't want to leave his job even if he was stinking rich. He picked the blue sapphire out of his pocket and smiled.

The mum was talking about carrying the kid back and the Dad was telling her he would do it. Jaimey passed the sapphire to the Dad and spoke without pausing. 'Hi. My name is Jaimey. I just stole this by mistake. There is going to be a huge reward for anyone who finds it. Or you could keep it. I don't mind. I just thought you could take it. I really don't want it. And they won't come looking for me. And they won't be angry at you if you give it back. Err. Okay?'

Bracq snapped out of his daze as Jaimey started to run off. The blue gem glistened in his palm. The sheer weight of it felt unreal. A fizzing pleasure began in his belly as he felt a million little tensions begin to unwind.

Fraser jogged back in to the museum. He nodded at an acquaintance who was directing guests and scanning details before shepherding them out the door. He walked through the holo barrier and felt a moment's satisfaction that his rank ensured the alarm did not sound.

He walked back towards the scene of the crime but stopped when he saw one red glistening shoe and the corner of a pale shoulder. Tuula was crouched down, holding a backpack tight to her stomach with tears threatening. She was biting her lip in determination, trying to hold back the flood.

'I should have been looking after him.' She whispered softly without looking up. 'I can't find him.'

'Hey it's okay –' Fraser started.

'He was so close when it fell. And I can't reach him. I'm

scared that –' Tuula's voice cracked as she held back a sob.

Fraser sat down next to her and toppled her over into his lap. 'They already scanned it. Nobody's under there.'

Tuula tried in vain for a few seconds to stop the flood of tears, but the weight of relief was a far more effective catalyst than the sickening dread and fear had been.

She made another effort to pull herself together when she realised she had no spare dry skin on her arms to wipe her face with.

'I swear I didn't know. I know you can't possibly believe me but it's true. You told me not to come and I did the exact opposite and I've been your suspect all along and now I'm right in the middle of it... I'm so sorry.' She pushed away from his chest to see what expression she had to contend with on his face. Not that it mattered. She was screwed.

Fraser smiled as he smoothed her hair and wiped away the last tear. 'You are certainly going to be hauled in for questioning...Again...By me.'

Tuula launched in to rapid speech again, 'I know. God I'm so sorry! It will be okay though. Nobody knew we –well, we never –' She slowed a little but started a new tack almost immediately 'You have been nothing but strictly professional with me and I can testify that to anyone.'

Fraser laughed. 'Yes look at my professional behaviour right now for instance!'

Tuula scrambled up and groaned. She clutched her hands as she whispered frantically. 'I'll speak to them. There's nothing on file or on the grid to implicate that we …' Tuula trailed off, unable to find a word for what they had been.

Fraser caught her hands in his and smiled down at her anxious face. 'Nothing to implicate that we …?' He prompted.

Tuula frowned. 'I mean you only came to my place. No-one knows about that. And all the other times you were just interviewing me for the thefts. So no-one will know that I –'

Fraser cupped her face and kissed her on the mouth. He leaned back leisurely, smiled and lifted an eyebrow, 'No-one will know that you…?'

Tuula ransacked her mind for a suitable reply and found under his intense gaze that it had turned to mush. 'Umm.'

'My little robin, lost for words I see.' Fraser shook his head and grinned. 'Don't tell me you skipped debating club in that school of yours?'

Tuula started to turn away and Fraser took pity on her. He turned her back and kept a light hold on her shoulders, checked they were still unobserved and whispered back, 'I've been listening in to the comms all night. Your brother has made what is known in the profession as a 'clean getaway'. And quite a convenient one at that.' He paused to kiss her again, 'and as my best friend and colleague is willing to perjure himself in order that I can continue to –' Fraser paused elegantly and smiled, 'love you, I think we can forget the need to obliterate our relationship in the eyes of the law.'

'But!' Tuula gasped before being enveloped in a giant hug. 'You love me? Honestly?' She managed a shaky smile.

'Uh huh.'

'Do you know how long I've been trying to supress it, thinking you were just playing with me? You are – so – unfair!'

Fraser smiled and kissed her again, thoroughly scattering her thoughts. 'Did you honestly think I needed to see you that many times for one investigation? Don't you know how lazy lawmen are?' He laughed 'Just promise me one thing…'

Tuula smiled 'Anything.'

'I really do think your family is going to have to quit the world of theft. I am reasonably au fait with deception and concealment but there is a limit to my talent'

Tuula leaned in to his warm chest and sighed, 'I haven't seen any limits yet.'

ABOUT THE AUTHOR

Anna Lawrie was born in England but spent a lot of her childhood in Wales where she learnt the incredibly useful skill of reversing back up one in two inclines in the dark.

She now lives in Kent with her husband, two children and various animals, and wedges in her writing between volleyball, school runs, running a Physiotherapy department and tending a vegetable plot with intermittent success.

Printed in Poland
by Amazon Fulfillment
Poland Sp. z o.o., Wrocław